Promiscuous

By
Missy Johnson

ISBN: 978-0-9924665-9-6

First Printing: February 2014

Missy Johnson

ISBN-10:0992466598
ISBN-13:9780992466596

Other books by Missy

Provoke
Seduce (A Beautiful Rose Prequel)
Beautiful Rose (Beautiful Rose #1)
Captivating (Beautiful Rose #2)
Tease (Tease #1)
Promiscuous (Tease #2)
Always You
So Many Reasons Why
Incredible Beauty
Desire
Inseparable

Social Media

Email: missycjohnson@gmail.com
Twitter: @MissycJohnson
Facebook: www.facebook.com/MissycJohnson

Prologue

Beth

Fucking Coop.

I was so pissed off at him. We had arranged drinks for tonight *weeks* ago, and he just didn't show up? A short text, half an hour later, explaining that Mia was jealous of our friendship was not fucking good enough. No call. Not even an apology.

And as if that wasn't bad enough, Ivan, my manager, just *happened* to be at the same bar I was? I wouldn't put it past him to follow me. That was just the kind of creepy, weird thing he'd do.

It wasn't the first time I had seen him when I was out. I was sure my reputation as a party girl was behind it.

Maybe he thought if I got drunk enough, he could be there, waiting . . .

And what do you know, he had been. I'd barely finished reading Coop's rejection text when there was Ivan, a drink in hand. I'd been too annoyed at Coop to turn down a free drink, even if it meant putting up with Ivan's company for a bit.

"What's a pretty little thing like you doing all alone?" He smirked. He pushed the drink along the bar, his stubby fingers tapping on the counter. "You haven't been stood up, have you, Bethy?"

Ugh. The mocking tone of his voice made me cringe. He eyed me, every inch of me, from my curled blonde hair down to my black stilettos.

"My *friend* couldn't make it," I replied. I kept my voice cool, hoping he'd get the message. He didn't, and I shuddered as he chuckled to himself.

"Good thing I'm here then, huh?"

No, not really. All I wanted was Coop, but unfortunately he had deserted me. I sighed and downed the rest of my drink, much to the delight of Ivan. He reached for the empty glass. I jumped as his fingers brushed over mine slowly and deliberately. His lips cracked into a smile, revealing his hideous, yellowing teeth, which made my stomach turn.

"I'll get you another," he murmured, smacking his lips together as his beady little eyes openly gazed at my chest.

"Sure," I said dully, my mind still on Coop.

A few drinks later, I'd had enough. Standing up, I reached for my jacket, Ivan's fingers brushing past my arm.

"Leaving so soon?"

"It's been a long day," I muttered.

"I was just leaving too."

I eyed his near full glass of beer and raised my eyebrows. He chuckled and stood up.

"Let me give you a lift. I've got some papers that need your signature in the car anyway."

In my gut I *knew* it was a bad idea, but I was so angry

at losing my only real friend that I'd just wanted to get home as quickly as possible. As much as I disliked Ivan, I'd known him for years; I never thought he would actually try anything.

Only, I hadn't expected him to follow me up to the door, or push his way inside my home. He waved a handful of papers at me.

"Contracts," he said in his slight Irish accent, dampened by ten years spent living in the U.S. He grinned as he ran his fingers through his curly, ginger hair. My stomach back-flipped as I nodded, trying to mask how uncomfortable his attention was making me.

I stood on the other side of the sofa, as far away from him as possible. My hands twitched nervously behind me as I took in his tall, wiry frame. I don't know why, but tonight he was creeping me out more than usual. For Ivan, that was a hard task. He was always a first-class weirdo, but tonight there was something more than just his usual creepiness. The look in his eyes . . . I shuddered, and the tiny hairs on the back of my neck stood up and sent shivers down my spine. My breathing began to shallow. I couldn't explain it—even when I wasn't looking at him, I could feel his eyes on my body.

He slowly inched toward me as my instincts kicked in, telling me I *needed* to get away from him.

"Just leave them on the coffee table and I'll have a look over them tomorrow."

"Okay then." He threw the papers down on the table, his brown eyes not breaking away from mine as he continued to move toward me.

"Uh, so, I'm kind of busy. I'll see you tomorrow. Thanks for the lift home," I muttered. I was done trying to be nice; I just wanted him gone. The sooner he left, the sooner I could end what had been a hell of a day with a hot bath, and sleep off the several drinks I'd consumed.

I tugged at the hem of my short, red dress as Ivan's eyes lingered on my legs before very slowly moving up and over my body. I hated the way he leered at me, as if I were a piece of meat.

He walked towards me, his grin widening. I tensed and backed up until he had me pressed against the wall with nowhere to go. I swallowed, a lump forming in my throat as he reached out and touched my stomach.

The feel of his fingers running down the soft silk of my dress made me cringe. I tried to get away. I tried to maneuver my way from under him, but his arm shot out against the wall. I was blocked in. His weight was up against me. He was so close I could feel how aroused he was. As he surrounded me, his intentions becoming clear, I began to panic.

Oh no. Please don't let him do this.

I tried again to move, but I was locked into this space like a prisoner in a tiny cell. He had a good six inches and at least fifty pounds on me. He wasn't that well-built, but compared to my hundred-pound frame, he might as well have been a wrestler.

"Come on, Beth. Is that any way to show your appreciation to a friend who helped you out of a *tight* spot?"

"Let me go," I yelled as I struggled to free myself.

He smiled, exposing those grotesque teeth, and pressed me harder against the wall. "Don't be like that, Beth. I don't like games, and you've been playing me for a while now, you little cock-tease."

He grabbed hold of my neck as I tried to break away from him. Pain shot through me as his grip on me tightened, his nails digging into my skin so hard I could feel my blood pulsate against the pressure of them. A cry escaped me as he groped at my breasts and forced his mouth against mine. I coughed, gagging at the taste of his rancid breath.

He's going to rape me. Bile began to rise up in my throat. I tried to scream. "Why are you doing this?" I sobbed, the salty taste of tears running onto my lips.

He didn't answer. Instead, he grabbed hold of my forearm and pulled at it roughly. I gasped, his strength winding me. With one more hard yank, we tumbled to the floor. I landed hard. He hovered over me. He was way too strong, and in complete control.

H' weight crushed down on me as I struggled to 's dark eyes, now overshadowed with rage, on mine as he gripped both my wrists together m above my head while his other hand roughly pushed my dress up, exposing me.

"Please," I sobbed as his hand groped between my thighs. I kicked frantically, desperately trying to free myself. I gasped as his fingers brushed my panties aside before they roughly and forcefully thrust inside of me. I felt sick, and at the same time, like this wasn't real. It couldn't be. I'd *never* let this happen. I was disgusted at *myself* for putting myself into this situation.

"Don't do this. Please, Ivan, *stop*," I yelled, struggling to free my hands.

He grunted in response. It was almost a laugh. His hand curled around my black lace panties, and with a sickening rip, they were off me. Pain shot through my legs where the fabric had burned into my skin. A fresh lot of tears ran down my cheeks as I began to weaken.

This can't be happening. Please… please no.

My heart dropped as I heard the sound of his zipper and then felt his fumbling between my legs. Another wave of nausea ripped through me as I braced myself for what was next.

"No!" I shrieked, trying with my last ounce of strength to free myself.

But he was just too big, his grip on my wrists so tight I was beginning to lose feeling in my fingers. I cried out as his fist connected with my face. My eye throbbed. My vision became cloudy as my eye began to close over. I bit down on my lip so hard I tasted blood.

"Stop fighting this, Bethy," he whispered in my ear.

I cringed, the stench of body odor and stale cigarettes enveloping me. I whimpered as he forced his fingers inside me again and moved them around.

"Ooh, you're nice and wet for me baby."

"Stop…please stop."

"You can have me for free, honey. No need to go paying for it," he whispered in my ear as his fingers groped roughly inside of me. All I could do was lie there and beg like a fucking puppy—beg him not to do what he had every intention of doing, what he was already doing. Plead with him not to take the only thing I'd had control over my entire life.

He removed his fingers and forced himself inside, the pain leaving me breathless. I choked back tears as he fondled my breasts, his hands all over me like he had a right to my body. I squeezed my eyes shut and focused on the sound of my heartbeat. I tried to block everything else out.

Bump, bump, bump, bump.

"You feel amazing. Better than I imagined, honey," he huffed as he thrust inside of me. "For a slut, you're really fucking tight. God, oh yeah. You like that? You like the feel of a real man inside you, honey?"

I didn't respond. Instead, I lay there shaking, and slowly dying inside as he moved inside of me. I gasped as his fist connected with my face again, crashing me back down to reality.

Please make him stop. Oh God, please just make him stop.

"Say it, Bethy. Tell me how much you want this. Fuckin' say it," he growled in my ear.

"I *don't* want it," I sobbed as he raised his hand to hit

me again. My eye had already closed over, and the pain I felt everywhere was unbearable. "You disgusting, fucked up excuse for a human being, I hope you rot in hell!"

He roared with laughter, my words having no impact on him whatsoever. "I've caught myself a feisty one," he grinned, licking his lips.

I closed my eyes, repulsed…disgusted.

Please, stop. Please just leave me alone . . .

"No!"

I cried out as he came inside me, the shame and worthlessness I was feeling breaking me. How could I call myself a strong woman when I let something like this happen to me? I should've fought harder. I should have stopped him. Why the *fuck* had I gone home with him? *Why?*

This was like my childhood all over again. My sister flashed into my head. All those years of torture at the hands of her scum boyfriends had come to an end the day I found her dead in the bathtub. She had overdosed. I was fifteen. Fifteen, and finally free. Fifteen and alone.

All that I'd accomplished since then meant nothing now as I lay crying on the floor, Ivan still inside of me.

He pushed me aside and got to his feet. I sat there, crying, my knees pressed up to my chest and my hands curled tightly around my legs, creating a barrier between him and me. He stood over me as he buckled up his pants, the satisfied grin matching the evil in his eyes.

Fucking asshole. Every part of me ached, yet the pure hate I felt for this piece of scum right then outweighed every other sensation.

"You should be grateful anyone still wants you after the way you acted with that escort. Then you go around dressed like that?" He laughed and threw something white in my direction. "You wanted this, and you know it. You're the biggest slut in this business." He winked at me and turned to leave.

As he reached the door, he abruptly turned back. "I don't need to tell you to keep this between us, do I? Nobody is going to believe you—not with my word against yours. And don't get any ideas about firing me, honey. I'll sue you into the fucking gutter for breaking our contract."

He laughed. "The gutter. Right where I found you, huh?"

I let my head fall to the floor and began to cry as he walked out the door. I spotted the small bag of white powder and reached out for it.

Coke. He *had* been on something.

I'd seen the signs before, over and over, with every piece-of-shit boyfriend my sister had let into our home. I racked my brain, trying to piece the night back together, trying to figure out what I could have done to prevent this. Was it my fault? *Had* I led him on? It played over and over in my head, like a scene stuck on repeat, a nightmare I couldn't break free from.

Wiping my eyes, I struggled to my feet, ignoring the burning pain and wetness between my legs. I clutched my right shoulder, which was aching from landing on it when he'd pushed me, and staggered to the bathroom.

The steam enveloped me as I climbed into the scalding-hot shower. Leaning against the wet tiles, I wrapped my arms around my stomach as loud sobs escaped from me. Why had I let him drive me home? I'd never felt comfortable around him. Letting him into my house was a stupid, stupid idea.

Fuck, Beth, what the hell were you thinking?

But that was the point: I'd been so focused on being annoyed at Coop that I *hadn't* been thinking. I couldn't tell the police, or anyone else for that matter, because he was right—it was his word against mine, and nobody was going to believe me.

"Leave me alone," I shrieked, scrubbing furiously at my skin. Blood, mixed with the warm water, began to pool on the shower floor. I examined my arms. I'd scrubbed so hard the skin had begun to break. And it still wasn't enough. I could still feel him. I could still smell him.

I could feel him everywhere. He was on me, he was inside of me . . . he was *everywhere*.

I doubled over and gagged, the bitter taste of bile and alcohol burning my throat. How could this have happened to me? As a teenager there had been many close calls, but never . . . nobody had ever gotten this far.

My knees gave way underneath me and I fell to the floor. Why? Why me? The loud sobs escaping from my mouth sounded so foreign, as if they were coming from someone else. But they weren't. It was all me. This had happened to *me*.

My body was the only thing I'd ever had control over. I'd never been a prude, but whom I slept with and when had *always* been my decision. Through all the uncertainty I'd experienced over the years, my right over my own body had been the only constant.

Now I didn't even have that.

* * *

I finally moved from the floor of the shower to my bed, but not before the water ran cold. Shivering, I fumbled for my phone, my hands trembling as I called Coop. No answer. I tried again and again; each time, the call rang out. I slammed it down onto the bed next to me, frustrated that he wasn't around when I needed him.

Every time I closed my eyes, the image of Ivan hovering over me would fill my head. So I lay there, alone, the faint light spilling from the lamp beside my bed my only source of comfort, until I eventually fell asleep.

***

The next twenty-four hours passed in a blur. I was either asleep, or crying, or running over what had happened in my mind. As soon as I'd fall asleep, I would wake up screaming, reliving the whole nightmare. Every time I closed my eyes, he was there, on top of me.

I couldn't get away from him, and what I hated the most was how easy it was to let Ivan's words creep inside my head. Maybe I had asked for it? And he was right— nobody would believe he'd raped me. I laughed bitterly. The press would love a story like this. *Bethany Masters Cries 'Rape.'*

He knew I wouldn't tell anyone—he knew that before he raped me. My decision not to report him would have shocked some people, maybe even angered them, but from my perspective there was no point. I was convinced that this was somehow my fault, and I had nobody on my side to tell me otherwise.

My phone beeped, scaring the hell out of me. Panting heavily, I collected it from the bed next to me and read the message. It was from Coop.

Shit, Beth, I'm sorry about yesterday. Everything is all good now, I promise. Come over for dinner tonight, okay? I really want you and Mia to be friends.

I snorted angrily. Everything was okay. Well, thank fucking God he thought everything was fine. He hadn't just been raped. His whole world wasn't collapsing around him. Tears stained my cheeks as I tapped back a response.

Sure, whatever. See you tonight.

Switching my phone off, I rolled over, snuggling down into the familiarity of my blankets. My body ached more today, and my head was pounding—probably from all the crying. Large blue and purple bruises had begun to surface on my thighs and my arms. I was a freaking mess, and in no condition to go out anywhere. All I wanted was someone to comfort me, someone to tell me things were going to be okay.

I needed *him*. I needed him, alone with me, but that wasn't an option.

And right now, there was only one thing worse than

the thought of spending the night with Coop and Mia.

And that was spending the night alone.

***

I banged repeatedly on the huge wooden door until it swung open. My face broke into a grin.

"Coop," I yelled, collapsing into his arms. If he hadn't opened the door at that very moment, I probably would've collapsed into it. I was so sleepy. I glanced around the hallway of Coop's place as the room began to spin out of control.

Oh, shit. This isn't good.

"Beth? Are you feeling okay?" Coop asked, carrying me inside. "What the fuck happened to your face?"

I giggled and gazed up at him. *God, look at those eyes.*

"I'm okay, Coop. Just loosening up," I muttered, and struggled out of his arms. His strong, sexy arms... I unbuttoned my jacket.

"Coop, where shall I put this—" Jake stopped

midsentence, his jaw dropping to the floor. He stood there, a bottle of wine in his hand, gaping at me as I tossed the jacket onto the sofa. I glanced down and giggled. *Oopsie.* I'd forgotten to get dressed.

"Jake," Coop said urgently. He grabbed my jacket and threw it around me. "Do not let either of them in here. I'm taking Beth home."

Jake, still frozen to the spot, didn't respond.

"Jake!"

He snapped back to reality, and nodded. "Okay, go." He threw his keys to Coop. "Take my car. I'm just out front."

Coop led me out to the car. I sighed, happy that he was there for me. I felt so much better when he was around me. *Protected.*

"Beth? Can you tell me what you've taken?" he asked, shaking me gently.

Opening one eye, I looked at him, embarrassed. My face heated up as I slowly remembered what had happened.

All I wanted to do was sleep and never wake up.

"Just some coke. No big deal . . ." I mumbled, slipping into darkness.

"What's wrong with her?"

"She told me she took some cocaine."

"Come with me. The more you can help me, the better your friend will be."

"Now, what's your friend's name?"

"Bethany Masters."

***

My eyes fluttered open, the glaring light from above almost blinding me. Coop sat next to the bed. I swallowed and looked away; I couldn't stand to see the pity in his eyes.

"I'm sorry, Coop."

"What the hell, Beth? Since when do you do drugs?"

His voice came out harsh, laced with anger and frustration.

I cringed, not in the mood to explain. I didn't care. I shrugged weakly. "It was stupid. I'm sorry."

"No, you don't get to blow me off. You've been acting weird since yesterday. Are you angry at me for last night?" He leaned over, running a finger softly over one of my bruises. "Who did this to you, Beth?"

I shook my head as warm tears splashed my cheeks. "Just leave it, Coop. Please." I rolled over so he wouldn't see me crying. "Please go. And don't contact me anymore, okay?"

"What?" he said incredulously. He twisted my body until I was facing him, confusion flashing in his eyes.

"Go," I yelled. "Get out!" I held my breath and waited until I could hear his footsteps fading away.

Chapter One

Beth

Two months later…

The pretty blonde smiled at me as she leaned against the wall, her fingers lingering on my hip. Her deep green eyes caught mine as her hand wandered up the curve of my almost-bare back before wrapping around my neck and pulling me in. Her lips, so soft and feminine, crushed me as her manicured nails dug into the base of my head. I kissed her back, the faint scent of cherry lip-gloss hitting my nose as my tongue curled around hers.

The small crowd of mostly men that had gathered next to us cheered as we kissed, a few wolf whistles echoing over the pounding music. Spurred on by the attention, my hands roamed over the top of her skimpy silk tank, following the curves of her breasts as I gave the boys a show. Another round of cheers erupted as my hand moved under her top, my fingers dipping into the cup of her bra as she giggled and kissed me again.

"Take it off!" someone yelled. Out of the corner of my eye, I spotted a small group of women standing near the bar, whispering and pointing at us. I rolled my eyes.

Being a twenty-year-old pop star, if they weren't talking about you, then you were old news—and people were *always* talking about me. A girl-on-girl experience is practically a rite of passage in the world of pop. If you didn't do it at least once, you weren't doing things right. And if you didn't do it at all, they'd most likely make it up anyway, so why the hell not?

I wasn't really into girls, but it felt good to wind the boys up, and apparently nothing did that better than making out with another chick. I could hear the sound of clicking cameras in the distance, and I knew this would probably end up on the front page of some magazine tomorrow.

Bethany Masters' Lesbian Romp.

But who really gave a damn? I didn't.

I'd tried being the good girl, and nobody had cared—least of all *him*. The gossip columns were forever making things up about me, so it wasn't like I actually had a reputation to ruin. And besides, being bad felt good. It dulled the pain of losing him and . . . the rape.

I shuddered, Ivan's face flashing through my mind. Having to see him every day was hard—the way he looked at me, like he had won. All reporting him would have done is give him the satisfaction of everyone knowing what had happened, or at least what I claimed to have happened. It was hard enough to prove a rape without all my history. Sucking it up and moving on was *my* way of not letting him win.

But that didn't stop the nightmares, or the pain I felt, or that every time I closed my eyes he was what I saw, over me . . . inside me.

This? Going out, getting drunk, and acting up?

This was how I coped. Alcohol fixed everything. It took away all those niggling little thoughts in the back of my head that reminded me of that night. Alcohol transformed me from the scared, vulnerable girl I had become into someone with no problems and no inhibitions. Without it, I don't know how I'd have survived the past two months. Who cared what effect it was having on my life? Getting through each day was all that mattered. It stopped my every thought from going back to how Coop had deserted me when I'd needed him most.

In his defense, our relationship hadn't exactly been normal: I'd been paying him for sex. Somehow, I'd fallen hard for him; then he'd fallen for some other woman, and I'd been left with nobody. I could've gotten past that, but we were supposed to have been friends. Friends don't treat each other the way he'd treated me. The moment she felt insecure about his friendship, he'd cut me off. I'd been there for him when he'd needed help, and it hurt that he hadn't done the same for me.

Fuck him. I didn't need anyone. I'd handled the five years before him on my own, so I sure as hell could handle myself now.

***

"Here we go," I yelled to the cheering crowd as I downed another shot. The liquid burned as it slid down my

25

throat, the buzz from the alcohol filling my head, blocking out everything else.

"Come with me?" Blondie asked coyly, her hand slipping into mine.

I hesitated and then nodded. "Sure, just give me a sec." I waded through the crowd toward the bathroom. I needed to be alone. The panic attacks didn't come often, and my usual way of treating them was with more alcohol. Pushing though the heavy bathroom door, I staggered up to the sinks.

I stared at my reflection in the mirror. I'd dyed my long auburn hair a dirty blonde after the rape. Coop had loved my hair—that's why it had to go. Seeing it had reminded me of how in love with him I still was.

Maybe I should've gone black. It would have suited my mood, and royally pissed Ivan off. Or better yet, I could shave it all off. I sniggered at the thought.

My green eyes stared back at me, void of emotion, almost dead. I rifled through my clutch for my mascara and brushed a thin layer over my lashes. Reaching for my phone, I saw a message from Coop. I sighed as I opened and read it.

Will you please fucking answer my messages? I'm worried about you. I'm sorry that I didn't answer your call before, but I'm here for you now, Beth. I don't want to lose you. Please, just let me know you're okay. Wherever you are, I'll come get you, and take you back home.

He's worried about me? I snorted. *Fuck you, Coop.* And how the hell did he know I wasn't at home? Was he following me now? Anger boiled up inside me as I slammed my fist down on the white marble surface.

Ignoring the pain shooting through my wrist, I shut off the phone and shoved it back in my purse, trying to pretend his words hadn't affected me. But they had. They always did. I felt the tears welling up, but I tossed back those emotions. I refused to cry. I needed to feel *nothing*, because the moment I opened that door and let myself grieve, I wasn't sure how I would go on.

The last time we'd spoken had been almost two months ago now, and since then, every day he'd sent a message or tried to call. But I just couldn't handle it. I

couldn't *be* his friend. Not right now. Why the hell hadn't
he gotten the message?

***

I splashed water on my face, the cold snapping me
back to the present. Taking a deep breath, I ran a sheet of
paper towel over my cheeks and walked back into the club,
moving through the masses of bodies back to Blondie.

The Marz Bar was where you hung out to be seen. Full
of stars and wannabes, it was a place that would definitely
get you noticed. This place crawled with paparazzi just
waiting for the shot that would push them into the big
league. Not surprisingly, I had a trail of them following me
and the blonde as she led me into the VIP area at the back
of the club.

Two tall and muscly security men stood guarding the
entrance. Both wore a menacing expression, which made
me confident that there was no chance of anyone who
shouldn't be there sneaking through. I eyed the men as
Blondie led me past them. The giant bear on the right gave
me a sly grin, so I dropped my gaze to his crotch and licked
my lips. He shuffled uncomfortably, which made me

giggle. Men were so damn easy.

What exactly was I doing? No idea. I was more than slightly sloshed, and a little bit horny. As I said, women usually weren't my thing, but the way Blondie's tight, black dress was riding up her perky little ass was making me frisky. Alcohol gave me a glimpse of the old Beth. I can't explain the relief, knowing she was still in there . . . somewhere.

Inside the VIP area, Blondie pushed me up against the wall, her hands cupping my breasts as she began to lick my neck.

"You feel like a little fun?" she muttered, her lips working their way down beneath the thin fabric of my low-cut dress. I smiled, moaning in response. She led me down the hall and into an empty room. My eyes darted from the leather sofa that lay against the back wall to the private bar in the corner and back to Blondie, who was grinding herself against me.

I didn't see him at first. I was too busy trying to tug that damn dress off her.

My first realization that we weren't alone was when I

felt him—behind me. His hands ran over the curves of my hips. I jumped back, my body pressing into his. I should've been scared—hell, this whole situation should have terrified me—but there was something calming about his presence and the way he was touching me. I stepped back further, the alcohol driving my confidence as I began to grind my hips into his crotch.

"You did well, Scarlett. Very well," he murmured in my ear as he hardened against my ass. His voice was deep and smooth, like the finest chocolate. The blonde began to smile, enjoying the praise. She lifted her dress over her shoulders and let it fall to the floor, then undid her bra, her rounded breasts bouncing out of containment. I eyed her, my mouth drying up as a familiar feeling stirred in my stomach. I know I said I wasn't into chicks, but God help me, if I were . . .

Slowly, he turned me around. This whole experience was beginning to get *very* hot very fast, and was exactly what I needed. I'd come here tonight looking for something, and I was convinced this was it.

His arm slipped around my waist as I looked up into the deepest pair of brown eyes I'd ever seen. They almost looked as though they were melting. Or maybe I was melting into him.

He was quite possibly one of the most attractive men I'd ever seen, albeit a little older than the boys I was used to playing with. Coop had been twenty-five, but this guy had to be in his mid-thirties—almost twice my age. But his age had no effect on how attractive I found him.

That dark hair—cropped short, but still with the slightest wave to it—and the way his lip curved up on one side when he looked at me made me wet. His tie was loosened with the top two buttons of his white shirt undone, and his charcoal pants did nothing to hide how well equipped he was, especially in his excited state. My head began to spin as I inhaled his scent, musky and sweet. I just wanted to lick him . . . among other things.

My heart began to race as his fingers traced my hairline, then down my neck and over my collarbone. They stopped just short of my chest, waiting, as his gaze burned into me. There was something so confident about this man . . . *He's irresistible*.

I knew nothing about him, yet I *needed* him. He was

the key to allowing me to forget, at least for one night. I needed to use him to erase the hounding thoughts in my head.

Blondie pressed up against me and I jumped again. Disappointment rushed through me as I remembered we weren't alone. I'd forgotten about her.

I tilted my neck as she kissed me, my eyes never leaving his. He nodded at Blondie, who walked around in front of me as he sat down, his leg crossing over his knee, his arms stretched out over the back of the sofa.

"He wants to watch us," she whispered in my ear, her hands roaming underneath the hem of my dress, riding it up.

Hell, I'll give this guy whatever he wants.

I turned toward her and lifted my lips to hers. We kissed, her mouth pressed against mine, the softness of her skin so sexy and unusual. It felt so erotic making out with another girl. Kissing a guy was always so rough and raw. There was none of that here; it was all gentle and slow. Oddly, I found it just as arousing.

Unzipping the back of my dress, I lifted it over my head as Scarlett sat down on the plush leather sofa opposite him. He was looking at me as my dress fell to the hardwood floor in a heap. From either the cool breeze sneaking through the open window, or under his gaze, I began to shiver. My nipples ached against the constriction of my bra. I longed to give myself to this man. I wanted his mouth on every inch of my body. Moving toward Scarlett, I stumbled over my heels.

She held out her hand to steady me as I sat down on her lap, one leg on either side so I was straddling her, giving him a perfect view of my ass. My back was to him, but I could feel his eyes burning into me.

Scarlett lifted her arms around my neck and pulled me down to her, our lips entangling in a deep, slow kiss. With one hand holding the back of my neck, the other began to trail down my body. I moaned as her fingers moved over my strapless black bra and down past my stomach, finally resting on the damp lace fabric between my legs. I was wet. So wet. I never thought I could be this turned on by another woman, but she was beautiful, and doing this with her in front of him was almost enough to make me lose control.

I breathed in sharply as her fingers thrust inside of me, pushing aside my thong like it had no business being there. My grip on her shoulders tightened as she explored me so intimately, her eyes flashing with excitement and determination, like my pleasure was her only goal.

I moaned softly, my body jerking to the rhythm of her fingers, desperate for more of her, as much as she would give me. For a moment I almost forgot about him, but then the memory of those insanely sexy brown eyes came flooding back to me like a giant wave crashing over a bed of rocks.

"How does she feel, Scarlett? Is she wet for you?" His deep voice cut through me.

Scarlett nodded, her fingers continuing to thrust inside me as she held my gaze.

"She's wet. She's very wet. And so soft, too." She bit her lip as she pulled me in for another kiss. A little whimper escaped from me, and all I could do was try my hardest not to scream in ecstasy as this tiny little blonde beauty with perfect little breasts finger-fucked me out of this planet, with one of the hottest men I'd ever seen looking on.

Was he palming himself as he watched us? The thought of him sitting there fisting his hard cock as he watched her fingers move in and out of me had me ready to explode. I couldn't hold on much longer, no matter how badly I wanted this feeling to last forever.

And then it happened: I began to orgasm. A strangled cry escaped from my lips as I wrapped my arms around her neck, my pussy begging her fingers to delve deeper.

"Keep going, yes," I cried as her fingers circled around my clit. I wanted more, and I needed her to stop. I couldn't handle it, but oh God, how I *needed* it. Clenching my thighs, I forced her to finish, every part of me throbbing, aching.

Holy fuck, that was incredible. I fell onto my back, my head resting on the arm of the sofa, and my legs sprawled out over Scarlett. I met his gaze. His eyes burned into mine, a look of longing etched across his beautiful face. My eyes traveled downward to the huge bulge in his pants. I was surprised. He'd sat there that entire time and not gotten himself off.

I smiled lazily at him as Scarlett's fingers trailed over my legs, the pressure of her nails on my skin almost bringing me to another orgasm. He watched me intensely as I played with my nipples, trying to make him squirm. He held his own, though, his left eyebrow lifting as a sly grin spread across his mouth.

"Scarlett. You can go now." She stood up and nodded, quickly dressing. I looked from her and back to him, almost in awe at the allure of mystery he oozed. He intimidated me. I was used to men falling at my feet, but he was different. He made me feel less in control than I *needed* to be.

Scarlett scampered out of the room, leaving me alone with him. He walked over to me, his fingers running down my collarbone and over my panties. I breathed in sharply. Why did he have such an effect on me? He'd barely touched me, yet this was the most sensual experience of my entire life.

"So," I asked, slipping my dress back over my head. "Are you going to tell me what all this was about?"

"What do you mean? You looked like a girl who was

after a little fun, so I provided you with some entertainment." He smirked. I was more turned on than I had been with almost any other guy in my life, and he had barely put a hand on me.

"Hmm, I think I was the one providing the entertainment." I grinned. "And it looked to me that I wasn't the only one getting a little excited." I made a point of glancing downward.

He laughed and shook his head. "What can I say? I appreciate the female form. What man wouldn't be turned on watching two women? But this wasn't about me, Beth." God, the way he said my name made my knees weak. "Let me take you home," he murmured, reaching for my hand.

Holy mother of God. Had he felt that or was it just me? Maybe it was the alcohol; I *was* pretty buzzed. I nodded mutely. It seemed I'd lost the ability to speak in his presence.

In the back of my mind, I told myself that letting some guy I'd only just met drive me home from a club may not have been the smartest move, *especially* after Ivan, but my mind wasn't really in control of me right then.

If it were, it would have been screaming, *"How does he know your name?"*

Right at that moment, those mesmerizing brown eyes had full control over me.

Chapter Two

Beth

He pulled up outside my house, waiting for me to open the gates before completing the drive up to the front door. Thinking back, alarm bells should've been ringing—*this guy knew my address*—but the events of the evening were still playing over and over in my mind, and that tiny warning slipped from my thoughts like a speck of dust lost in a windstorm.

"Thanks for the lift," I whispered, not ready to move. His head cocked to the side and he stared at me, his hand working its way over to my thigh. I breathed in sharply, my skin tingling.

Please kiss me.

I know what you're thinking: Why the hell would she let a guy she barely knows drive her home from a bar a month after being raped? I'd be screaming the same thing at me. I honestly cannot tell you what I was thinking, only that I wasn't thinking clearly.

This was typical Beth behavior. Who reacts to a sexual assault with more sex? Apparently, I did. According to the internet, I should have been withdrawing from contact with people after an assault, but what I was feeling was just the opposite.

All my life, sex had empowered me. It gave me control over something, and I loved that. Fuck Ivan for taking that away from me. I was so desperate to cling onto that tiny thread of *me* that I'd somehow become even more sexual after the rape—if that were even possible. Only, I couldn't do it alone; I couldn't block out the memories without a whole lot of alcohol.

I didn't give a damn how people thought I should behave. I used to enjoy the feeling sex gave me, and I was obsessed with not losing that. If I lost that, then what did I have? I was stuck in a job with a manager who had raped me; I had no friends, no family, and no life. My life was a joke. I wasn't after sympathy, and the last thing I wanted was pity. Thinking about it made me depressed, so I distracted myself the only way I knew how.

"I'll come in with you, make sure you're safe."

He got out of the car and walked around to my side as I giggled uncontrollably. No doubt about it, I was drunk. I tried my best to look desirable as he helped me up the steps to the front door, catching me before I fell on more than one occasion. I'd be thinking back on this the next day and cringing, but I was doing a lot of that lately, anyway.

"Do you want me to tuck you in?" he asked, his smoldering eyes laughing at me.

I fumbled with my keys and turned to him with every intention of glaring, but what resulted was a giddy smile. "I'll be fine, thank you," I replied, tossing my long blonde hair over my shoulder. I stumbled inside as he stood on the porch, shaking his head, amused.

"Thanks for getting me home safely," I said, balancing against the doorframe. Before I could think about it, I stepped forward and kissed him. He raised his eyebrows, a smile appearing on his sexy lips, which had been as soft as

I'd imagined them to be.

A wave of nausea rushed over me. *Here we go.* This was about the time I began to regret drinking so much. In about an hour I'd be swearing off alcohol for life, and then the cycle would begin again tomorrow.

"Are you sure you're okay?" he asked, his eyes creasing with concern. "You're looking a little . . . green."

I wanted to say yes. I wanted to tell him I was fine, and that he could leave, because the last thing I wanted was for him to see what I knew was coming. And if I didn't hurry up and get rid of him, it would be coming up all over his polished black leather shoes.

"I'm fine. 'Night . . ." My voice trailed off as I realized I still didn't know his name.

"Goodnight, Beth."

I watched as he walked away, confused by what I was feeling, still no closer to knowing his name, and not in the least bit disturbed that he knew mine. This guy stirred up emotions inside me that I hadn't felt for anyone since Coop—feelings of attraction that I wasn't even sure I was ready for. Especially after . . .

I shuddered, bad memories flashing through my mind. The alcohol, the partying, the sex—it was all I had to help me forget. In my stupid head, all these things I was doing that were destructive to my life were my way of trying to get back the control he had taken from me. The more out of control I got, the more in control I felt. At least, that's what I told myself.

***

I crawled my way up the stairs and fell onto my bed, still fully clothed and reeking of vodka and cranberry juice. My stomach ached like crazy, as though the alcohol was slowly eating away at the lining.

The urge to vomit hit me. I jumped off the bed, making it as far as the tiled bathroom floor before the night's contents spilled out of me. I groaned and sunk to the tiles, curling my legs up under me, and began to cry.

"This has got to stop," I muttered, clutching my stomach. I didn't want to be this girl, but I didn't know how to get over . . . *it*. I acted tough, but underneath I was scared as hell, and so, so alone.

People were beginning to comment that I was acting differently. But maybe this was the real me. Maybe who they thought they knew was just a cover for the nightmare of a person I really was. I'd tried to escape my past before, yet I always seemed to end up back in a shitty situation.

If only Coop had met me that night like he'd promised. I grabbed my phone and clicked on messages. Nothing. I'd begged for him to leave me alone, but when he did, I just ended up feeling worse. I couldn't handle being around him, but the thought of not having him in my life was worse. I was walking a dangerous line. How long until he gave up and just cut me off forever?

Chapter Three

Roman

My heart raced as I drove away, my mind struggling to process everything I knew about this girl. I could still feel her lips on mine. I hadn't been expecting that, but holy fuck. I shook my head, speechless.

I'd been watching her in the club as she slowly began to unravel, as if she were determined to spin out of control. I'd been content to just sit back and observe, but she changed that when she started throwing herself at anything that moved.

Why was she hell-bent on fucking up her life? It didn't matter. That wasn't important. I'd kept her out of trouble. I'd kept her safe. Even if that had meant sitting there watching her fuck Scarlett. I groaned, my dick hardening just thinking about it. Thinking about *her*.

Even though I'd been expecting her in the club that night, seeing her in front of me . . . the last thing I needed was to be attracted to her. I had a job to do, and I was going to do it.

But fuck, she was incredible. I saw behind the woman she was trying to be—behind the facade—to the scared, vulnerable, lost girl who was crying out for help. There was something there that I just couldn't ignore. I couldn't sit back and watch her destroy herself.

***

I'd spent the best part of the last month watching this beauty. She had been so free-spirited and happy to begin with. And then something had changed. It had happened so damn suddenly, and I was determined to figure out why. This had begun as just another job, a favor to an old friend. Back in those days, I'd been mixed up in some pretty heavy shit. But I'd turned myself around, and had actually taken my life somewhere.

I was thirty-two, I had my own business, a nice place, and all the hard work of the last three years was finally paying off.

Sliding the gearshift into drive, I maneuvered the car around and headed home. It was about a fifteen-minute drive, depending on the traffic. It gave me time to think about things. This particular job was a big deal. Whoever was hiring Carlos had cash, and a lot of it. They also had a big investment in this girl. If I played my cards right, I'd end up with a big check at the end of all this—more than enough to cover the remaining loan back to Carlos.

With my history, banks weren't too forthcoming with their offers for lending me money. Having to settle for an under-the-table loan shark wasn't ideal, but it got me what I needed to get the place up and running. The only problem was, he wasn't so understanding if a repayment was even a minute late. I knew that from personal experience.

Yep, this one single job would set me up for life—providing I didn't fuck things up. I was pretty sure that getting involved with the subject of my investigation would be fucking things up pretty majorly.

But I was invested now, and I had to help her. Watching her slowly unravel from a distance had been something I'd been able to separate myself from. But now, after tonight? Not so easy. Now, she was a girl in trouble. A girl who I wanted to help, who I *needed* to help.

The only question was, how much was I willing to risk to save her?

Chapter Four

Beth

Groaning, I hit the alarm. Again. The high-pitched beeping had been piercing through my brain like a skewer for the best part of the last hour. The clock read seven. At least I think it said seven. It was hard to tell with the major blurred vision I had going on.

Kicking back the covers, I sat up.

Oh, crap. The room was spinning. I was sure I hadn't gotten that drunk the night before . . . had I? The image of him, last night, floated through my head. And Scarlett. And me doing Scarlett. I cringed. Okay, maybe I had overindulged.

As I got to my feet rather unsteadily, I began to

undress, taking off last night's clothes. I stank of vomit and stale booze. In other words, I was a hot mess.

After cleaning the puke off the bathroom floor, I took two Tylenol and got in the shower, leaning my back against the wall for support as I let the water drench me. I lathered my body up with soap, and then rinsed it off as my head slowly began to ache less.

Stepping out of the shower, I reached for a towel and wrapped it around myself. I studied my face in the mirror. My skin was red and blotchy, and dark circles overshadowed my eyes. The makeup crew was going to hate me today. I made my way down to the kitchen and put on a pot of coffee—extra-strength.

The thought of eating made me feel sick, so I settled on a glass of apple juice and my coffee. Black, no sugar. It took half the cup for me to begin to wake up properly, and even then things weren't good. This was exactly why I needed to get myself under control: these drunken late nights were ruining me. I couldn't remember the last time I'd felt this shitty.

Wait, that's right: yesterday.

Throwing on the first thing I pulled out of the closet—
a pair of black yoga pants and a blue tee—I dabbed a little
concealer under my eyes and brushed my hair. Grabbing
my bag and my keys, I rushed out the door, already running
late. If there was one thing everyone in the music business
hated, it was tardiness. Time was money, and even five
minutes behind schedule could mean thousands of dollars
at the end of the day.

***

"You want me to what?" I gawked at Ivan, sure I had
heard him wrong. He rolled his eyes and shook his head at
the director as if to say *here we go again*. As if I were some
kind of diva.

"Beth, don't pretend to be shy. You know sex sells. If
you're naked in the video, it will get more hype. And that
means more sales," he added. I hated that little
condescending sneer of his.

Who was I kidding? I hated *everything* about him.

"Besides," he added, leaning in, his voice still loud
enough for everyone to hear, "it's not like nobody here
hasn't seen that little body of yours." He put his hand on

my ass and squeezed as I cringed.

My face flushed. Ivan was a snake, and I wanted nothing more than to slap that grin off his face. Instead, I stood tall, aware that the rest of the production crew was watching us, waiting for me to react.

"Fine," I said through gritted teeth. I stalked off to my dressing room, annoyed at myself for letting him get to me. That little comment about my body had me furious. I tried to ignore the glances from the other crewmembers. I knew what was going through their heads: *Has she fucked him, too?*

Slamming the door shut, I ripped off my jacket, my phone falling to the floor. I bent down to pick it up. A message. *Coop.* When was he going to take the hint that I needed space?

Beth, please talk to me. I'm worried about you.

Worried about me? Tears welled in my eyes and threatened to ruin my makeup. I quickly wiped them away. Where the fuck was he when I'd needed him? I deleted the message and shoved the phone back in my jacket, trying to forget about him and that night.

Slowly, I undressed. I stared at my naked body in the mirror, analyzing my features. My thoughts wandered back to Ivan and what a disgusting pervert he was. I didn't doubt for a second that he would be taking a copy of the film home so he could jerk off to it. *Oh, God.* The thought made me want to throw up. He made my skin crawl.

Turning my attention back to Coop, I tapped out a reply, my fingers shaking so hard they were missing the keys.

Please, just stop worrying about me. I don't matter to you anymore. Move on with your life, and forget about me.

Shoving the phone into my bag, I stalked out of the dressing room in only my robe, trying hard to ignore the leering eyes of Ivan. I thought about him thinking about me, and again, I wanted to hurl. I couldn't even stand to be in the same room as him. Every glance, every sneer brought that night flashing back. My heart raced as I walked back over to the set. I curled my arms around my waist and waited for the producer to tell me what he wanted me to do.

I forced myself to focus on him. *Sam Squires.* I'd

worked with him on some of my previous shoots. We'd gotten along well. The fact that he was gay made being naked in front of him that little bit easier. The only eyes I worried about being on me were Ivan's, but it wasn't like I could order him out of the room. If only I could order him out of my life . . .

"Beth, I need you to enter from over there, drop the robe, and wrap yourself in the sheet."

I glanced at the mock-up bedroom, complete with a canopy bed made-up with cream-colored silk sheets, and I nodded. I could do this. I had to do this.

As I walked over to the edge of the set, I forced myself to focus on something else. The first thing that popped into my head was *him*. Saturday night. Scarlett.

The thought of not seeing him again made me feel nervous, which made no sense because I knew literally nothing about him. But there was something about him that drew me in. A connection. It wasn't lust, or attraction—at least, it wasn't only that. I couldn't even explain it, but it was deeper. I felt safe around him. I felt around him the way Coop had made me feel.

I wasn't stupid. I knew my head was trying to replace what I had with Coop with someone who made me feel just as safe. Coop had been such a big part of my life for so long—much more than he'd ever realized. For him, I was a client and a friend; but for me, he'd been my only real friend.

In this business, everyone wants something from you. People don't hang around with you unless you can give them something. Coop had been different. He saw the real me, and loved me for who I was instead of what I could do for him. That was why I'd helped him out with his mom's care. Despite my feelings for him, I did want him to be happy.

And he was. Happy in the arms of another woman. God, I sounded so juvenile. It was so easy to forget I was so young. I was only twenty, yet I'd been the person in charge of my life for as long as I could remember.

We ran through the acts for the clip, most of which involved me rolling around half-naked on the bed, trying to look sexy—which was very hard to do with Ivan standing on the corner of the set, a faint smile on his lips. I shuddered, chills running down my back, wishing I was anywhere but there.

"Roll the other way for me, Beth. Can you show a little more leg?"

I lifted the sheet higher, uncovering all of my left thigh. If I went any higher the sheet would be pointless. I glanced over at Ivan just in time to see him shove his hand in his pocket. He narrowed his eyes at me and grinned.

Was…was he *touching* himself? My eyes widened as I glared at him in disgust. His lip curled up and he grinned in response. *Oh my god, he is sick!*

"Beth, just a few more shots—maybe smile a little more?"

I turned back to Sam and nodded, determined to block Ivan out. But that was easier said than done. The fact that he would do *that*, here, in full view of everyone made me wonder what else he was capable of.

***

Several takes later, we wrapped things up, the video finished—apart from editing. At least from a producer's standpoint, today had been a good day. In spite of my partying, my pounding head . . . and Ivan, I'd managed to be professional, and fast.

As soon as the final take wrapped up, I rushed to the dressing room, the silk sheet still wrapped tightly around my body. Tying my long blonde hair back into a ponytail, I stared at my reflection in the dressing room mirror. Huge dark bags hung under my green eyes—eyes that, to me, appeared empty and lifeless. If the eyes were the entry into the soul, then I was in some serious trouble.

I scrubbed the heavy makeup off my face, and then brushed some lip-gloss onto my lips. I quickly shoved my things back into my bag, eager to get home and relax.

Everyone else had left. I liked to wait until I knew I was alone, because then I could avoid the mindless chitchat, pretending to be interested in other people's lives.

The old Beth used to love talking to people; she was happy and social. Me? I just wanted to be left alone.

"I can't tell you how sexy you looked up there, honey."

I froze, my body instantly recoiling at the sound of that voice. Through the mirror, my gaze met his.

Ivan.

His dark eyes were almost black as he approached me. Still frozen in shock, I tried to focus on my breathing, and not on the way my skin crawled as he touched my shoulder, memories I'd tried so hard to bury pushing back into my mind. I swallowed heavily, wishing I were anywhere but here, alone with him.

"Such a pretty girl, Beth. I'm lucky to have you."

You don't have me, I wanted to scream.

But I couldn't. I sat there, frozen, as his fingers ran over my neck. My mind flashed back to that night. Him, on top of me . . . so heavy. His breath had reeked of cheap whisky and stale cigarettes, and the overpowering stench of his body odor. I shuddered, remembering his laughter as he ignored my pleas, asserting that *I wanted it.*

"I get hard just thinking about you, honey. The number of times I've jerked off, imagining everything else I'd like to do to you."

His voice shoved me back to reality. I jerked away, pushing the chair into him. He looked up, his mouth falling open as I sprinted for the door, scooping up my bag in the process. He laughed.

"God, Beth, you're not still on about this, are you?" He shook his head, as though he were dealing with a child. "You were so drunk, honey. Whatever you think you remember, you've got it wrong. You were just as into it as I was."

I grabbed the door handle and yanked it open, desperate to get out of there.

"Stay the fuck away from me, Ivan," I spat. I was shaking so badly, but I refused to let him see how much he was getting to me.

He chuckled. "Gladly, honey. But just in case you get any ideas, remember what I told you, okay?"

I stalked off, holding my bag to my stomach, trying to calm myself down. Only once I was out of the building did I let the tears fall.

I never cried—not before the attack. But he had me

and he knew it. I was under contract to him for another two years. If I broke that, I'd lose all my money; worse than that, I'd lose it to *him*. It would be my word against his, and who was going to believe me?

Suck it up and deal with it.

I wouldn't let him win. I refused to crumble because of *him*. Or at the very least, I refused to crumble in front of him.

***

I climbed into the safety of my bed, clinging tightly to the sheets nestled safely up around my neck. I refused to cry again. I wasn't going to waste my tears on something I couldn't change.

So my life sucked. I could either continue to spiral down the hole I was heading, or I could do something about it. If I kept this up, then he'd win. And I'd probably be dead within the year. The reality was, it was up to me what happened from this point onward.

My phone vibrated next to me. I reached for it and saw it was another message from Coop. A surge of anger rushed through me. Was he ever going to give up? How the fuck could I get over this if he wouldn't let me forget?

Beth, I just want you to know I'm here for you. Whatever is going on, you don't have to do it alone.

I laughed bitterly. He was here for me? What a load of crap. I tossed the phone down on the floor and rolled over, staring at the wall. He couldn't help me. The truth was, nobody could. I was the only one who could get me through this.

But it was never that easy, was it?

Chapter Five

Beth

Maybe what I need is a day in bed. A day of nothing.

I lay on my bed, staring at the ceiling, hundreds of thoughts racing through my mind like tiny pieces of a puzzle that wouldn't quite fit together. I was still angry from the shoot the day before. And at Coop for—well, for the sake of being angry at someone.

Ever since Mia had come into his life, it had been one broken promise after another. She didn't like me, and I understood that. If I were in her position I'd probably feel the same way. But that night at the bar and the day after were the last straw: I'd needed him, and he hadn't been there for me. That hurt me more than anything else in my life had. Now, as much as I missed him, I couldn't put myself out there to be hurt again. That was why I drank.

Anything to block out the memories of that night. I knew I blamed Coop because I needed someone to blame. I had to let the anger out on someone. If I didn't, I'd go crazy.

Right now, he was the focus of my anger. I couldn't take that out on Ivan, and if I let it build up inside me I'd go crazy. It wasn't fair, but I couldn't control how I felt.

It wasn't Coop's fault Ivan had raped me. I just needed someone to blame.

It had been more than two months since the attack, and I wasn't coping. The one thing about me was that I'd always been good at masking my feelings. To those who didn't know me, I was just the same as I always was: the party girl who never stopped.

Only people who knew me well—not that there were many of them—weren't fooled so easily. Like Coop.

The thing that scared me most about people finding out was what they'd think of me. I stayed off the internet as much as I could, but sometimes I'd Google my name and read the comments about me. I was a slut. A whore—which was funny, because last time I'd checked, I'd never been paid for sex. I could only imagine what they'd say about me being raped.

There is no right or wrong way to deal with that kind of assault. In my head, I knew I shouldn't have to feel embarrassed about how I felt, and how I'd responded. This was my way of coping; if I didn't have that, then I had nothing. I wasn't going to let anyone tell me that my way of coping was wrong, but at the same time, I feared that response. Fuck anyone who thinks everyone should react the same way.

The night after the rape was the last time I'd seen Coop. I'd been invited over for dinner, and let's just say things got a little out of hand. Not that I remembered much. A few days in the hospital and I'd still told nobody, though the nurse had asked me if I'd been assaulted: there was bruising around my thighs that was consistent with an assault. I'd just laughed and told her I liked it rough. Not convinced, she had persuaded me to be tested for STDs and pregnancy. Thankfully, all came back negative.

That was the last time I'd ever touch coke. The first

and last. I knew it was messed up, but at that point all I'd wanted to do was forget. But coke . . . I'd seen what that shit could do to people.

***

Kicking back the covers, I got out of bed. It was after twelve—a respectable time to get up on one of my very few days off. I had a big day planned involving me, the sofa, and a handful of old movies. The freezer was well stocked with Ben & Jerry's, in case of an emergency.

As I poured the filtered coffee that had been brewing—since my housekeeper, Noni, had left—into a cup, the doorbell rang. I tightened my blue silk robe around my waist and walked across the tiled floor to the door. Peering through the peephole, I jumped in shock.

"You," I said, opening the door, my eyes widening as I took in the familiar, sexy man leaning against my doorframe. His dark hair looked windblown, and those deliciously rich brown eyes leveled against my own, almost brooding.

A blush crept to my cheeks as I remembered the other night, and then the fact that under my robe I was completely bare-ass naked. But it wasn't embarrassment I was feeling; it was excitement. I was happy he was on my doorstep. I'd been sure I'd never see him again after the other night.

"Hello. Sorry to drop by unannounced, but I wanted to check that you were okay, and I didn't have your number . . ." His voice trailed off apologetically, his gaze wandering over my bare legs and my short robe.

"Do you want a coffee?" I asked, standing aside.

"Only if I'm not interrupting anything."

I blushed again, wondering what the hell he thought he would be interrupting.

"It's my one day off. I'm spending it watching movies and eating ice cream," I confessed.

"Then I'll take you up on that coffee." He walked inside, and I shut the door behind him. My eyes traveled down to his ass. God, he looked good. Dressed in a pressed white shirt and black slacks, he was positively hot.

His dark hair fell onto his forehead, and looked out of

control in comparison to the rest of him. Stubble lined his jaw, and I had to resist the urge to touch it. There was nothing hotter than stubble, especially on an older guy. Coop had it, and I used to pick on him for it, but secretly it drove me insane.

Ah, Coop. I still struggled to go an hour without thinking about him. Even with this insanely attractive man standing in front of me, my mind always went back to him.

Why? Because it was easier to tell myself I was over him than to actually believe it.

I led the man into the kitchen and poured him a coffee. He took it, glancing around the room, his eyes glistening with approval.

"Nice place," he commented.

I loved my home. Way too big for just one person, my home felt like the only place I could really be me. Everyone saw me as they wanted to: party girl, homewrecker . . . slut. I was none of those things. I acted like I didn't care what people thought about me, but I did. I was human, and I had feelings. Words hurt me just like they did everyone else.

After the incident with Coop, and it coming out that I'd used his services, my reputation had gotten worse—if that were even possible. Nobody cared about the truth, or me. All they cared about was getting a good story or a compromising photo. The reality was, I cried myself to sleep most nights. I hadn't spoken to my family in years, and I had no friends. Yeah, sure, I was living the life.

At least here I could be me. I could lie around on my black suede sofa that backed up against the window overlooking the city. I'd lost count of the number of times I'd curled up in the darkness, taking in the city.

"Thanks," I replied. I felt awkward. The other night, kissing him. *Why was he here?*

We stood in the kitchen, me leaning against the kitchen counter, and him . . . well, he was staring at me, a little smile on his lips. It was the kind of look that made me feel flustered, like he knew something about me. And considering how little I remembered of the other night, it was entirely possible.

"So, let me guess, you were just in the area?" I smirked, taking a sip of my coffee.

"Actually, I was nowhere near the area. I just wanted to see you again." Well, he got points for honesty. The sight of me fucking a girl had obviously left an impression on him.

I was beginning to realize what this was: he wanted more of the party girl. He was here to see the Beth who stayed out all night drinking, kissing random girls and making out with handsome men.

Not me. Well, not the real me, anyway.

I slipped a finger through the tie of my robe, letting it fall open. I arched my shoulders, letting the material float down my shoulders. Goosebumps hit my arms as I stood there confidently. Inside, I was a screaming mess.

What the hell am I doing? What if he touched me? What if I freaked out?

Sure, I'd had plenty of sex since the rape, but none sober. I hadn't let anyone touch me without being completely smashed first.

He stared at me for a moment, his eyes wandering over my curves as time seemed to freeze. I couldn't read his expression, but the longer he stood there, watching me, the more I began to panic. Without saying a thing, he bent down and retrieved the robe, threading my arms back into it.

"I'm not here to fuck you, Beth." He spoke softly, his hands running over the soft silk of my robe, down my arms to my fingers. I jumped back, both relieved and confused.

Well, this is embarrassing.

I turned away so he couldn't see the violent red burning across my cheeks. How had I read that so wrong? What could he possibly want from me if it wasn't that?

"Why are you here, then?" I muttered, rubbing my fingers along my forehead. This was quickly turning into another experience I wanted to forget. But erasing him from my mind wouldn't be that easy.

"I told you," he said simply. "I wanted to see you again. I wanted to check that you were okay."

"You've met me once. I don't even know your name. And somehow, I doubt the impression could've left you wanting more," I said dryly, trying to shrug off the humiliation I was feeling.

He chuckled. "You'd be surprised."

Would I? Now I was even more confused.

"Roman. My name's Roman."

"Roman," I repeated, liking the way it rolled off my tongue. It suited him. "So you don't want to fuck me, then why are you here?" I repeated. *Just get to the point and then go, so I can die cringing.*

His eyes sparkled. He was amused. *Great, I'm glad one of us is.* Was he playing with me? Flirting? If this was his idea of chatting up a girl, then he needed some serious lessons.

"I never said I didn't *want* to fuck you, Beth," he drawled, walking over to the sofa and sinking down in it. He cocked his head and studied me. "Trust me, quite the opposite, really. I'd love nothing more than to drag you down to your bedroom and fuck you senseless all day." His abrasiveness caught me by surprise.

I stood there, my eyes wide, not sure how to respond.

Guys usually weren't this hard to figure out. I slowly walked toward him and sat down with enough distance between us that I felt I could relax. Slowly, the embarrassment was giving way to the need for me to know what he found so interesting about me.

I thought back to the club. My memory was foggy, but what I could remember was him sitting there and *just* watching. No participation, no self-action, nothing—just his eyes on mine as another chick fingered me.

"Okay. So you want to fuck me. But you're not *here* to fuck me," I said, running a hand through my long hair. God, I was *so* embarrassed.

He chuckled, his eyes narrowing in on me as he processed whatever it was he found so fucking amusing. His enjoyment of this was irritating the hell out of me.

"Roman, you seem like a decent guy, but I don't have time for games, okay? Tell me what you want, or get out of my house," I said tersely.

He raised his eyebrows, a wide grin invading his mouth, which only served to annoy me even more. "Do you always get what you want, Beth?"

"No," I answered truthfully. If that were the case, I wouldn't be sitting there with *him* right then. I'd be sitting there with Coop.

He didn't look convinced. "You strike me as the type of girl who goes after what she wants."

"I do. That doesn't mean it always works out how I want it to."

He nodded slowly, as if he hadn't considered that a girl like me might *not* actually get everything she wanted. Why was everyone so quick to conclude that my life was like this perfect little world where everything Beth wanted, she got?

My entire life had been one struggle after another, and yet I'd gotten through that. I'd made something of my life where many people would've failed.

It would have been so easy for me to go the other way. I could've ended up like my mother: hooked on crack and selling my body for next to nothing to get my next hit. But I didn't. I'd worked hard to make something of myself.

"You think you know me, Roman, but the truth is, you

don't. You see me like everyone else does—this spoiled little brat who gets whatever she wants." I laughed bitterly. "If you knew what I'd been through over the past . . . over my entire life, you'd know that I deserve what I have just as much as anyone else, and I've worked fucking hard to get where I am."

Roman sat forward. He reached out, his hand grasping my thigh as his eyes bored into mine. I sat there, frozen, confused by the conflicting emotions pouring through me. How the hell could him touching me have me feeling terror *and* desire?

"Beth, I'm sorry. I didn't mean to suggest that. I'm an idiot. I had no business assuming anything about you, because you're right, I *don't* know you." He cocked his head to the side, his eyes narrowing slightly. "But I'd like to change that."

"Why?" I asked, throwing my hands up in frustration.

"Why what?" His brow furrowed in confusion.

"Why are you so intent on getting to know me, Roman?"

"Because I see a scared, lost girl in need of someone. I'm not asking you to be with me, or sleep with me. All I'm asking is you let me be your friend. Let me help you."

I slouched back in my chair, feeling defeated. I still didn't know what his game was. And right now, I didn't have the energy to argue with him. Besides, he was right—I was alone, and I so desperately needed someone on my side.

"I don't need your help, Roman. You want to be my friend? Fine, but don't think you're going to be my shoulder to cry on."

"The thought never entered my mind," he promised dryly. "So, as newly-acquainted friends, can I take you out for lunch?"

I glanced down at my robe and slippers. "I'm not dressed."

"I'll let you change." He chuckled.

I gave him a dirty look, but stood up. "Fine," I muttered, marching down to my room, "but you're paying."

***

So the guy had taste.

We sat down at a table, tucked in the corner overlooking the water in one of the most exclusive restaurants in Manhattan. I eyed him suspiciously. Even I would struggle to get a table here, especially at such short notice.

"What?" he asked, pouring me a glass of water.

"Nothing," I mumbled. "What is it you do, exactly? This is a pretty exclusive restaurant. I'm just wondering how you managed to get us a table."

"Let's just say I know how to get my way into a few places others don't." He narrowed his eyes, and smirked at me when I blushed at his comment. If he was referring to me right then, he obviously didn't read the gossip. Apparently I offered easier access than—

"Would you like a wine?" he asked.

I nodded.

He ordered a bottle of Pinot noir. "So, tell me about

yourself."

"There's not much to tell," I admitted. "I'm actually a pretty boring person."

"I don't believe that for a second," he murmured.

A shiver ran down my spine as I watched his eyes sweep over me. Was that . . . excitement I felt? I glowered at him, embarrassed by the way my body was reacting to his attention.

"We all have our secrets, don't we? Little things that make us who we are. Things that set us apart from everyone else, both in good and bad ways." Roman smiled.

I wonder what secrets he's hiding?

"I guess you're right." He was, but I was also hesitant to share anything about myself with someone I'd known for two minutes, no matter how devilishly sexy he looked slouched in his chair across from me.

"So, then tell me something. Tell me something about Beth that nobody else would know."

"I hate drugs."

He looked as surprised as I felt. Where had that come from? He waited for me to continue.

"Most of my adolescence was spent living with my sister. She was hooked on some pretty heavy stuff. Coke, heroin . . . she overdosed when I was fifteen." I reached for the water, gulping down a mouthful. I'd shared much more than I'd been wanting to. Even Coop didn't know this shit about me.

"Wow. That must have been really rough," he said softly.

I shrugged. It had been, but it happened, and there wasn't anything I could do about it.

"Your parents?"

"Mom died when I was twelve. Cancer. Dad—hell, I've never even met him. Apparently he was some deadbeat who ran out when I was young."

"That's a lot for a child to deal with."

"It is. But going through what I have was a big part of getting me where I am today." Well, not so much messed-

78

up Beth. Or maybe my childhood had an effect on that too. Who knew? I pushed my chair back and stood up. "Bathroom," I explained, smiling at the confused expression on his face.

"Do you want me to order for you?"

"Sure. A chicken Caesar salad, thanks." I hurried off toward the bathrooms, the urge to pee coming out of nowhere. That's what I got for starting the day off with two coffees and a glass of wine.

"Beth?"

I froze in the hallway just up from the bathroom. *Please, no.*

"Beth. I . . ." Coop's voice trailed off. He shook his head, clearly shocked to see me. "I can't believe it's you."

"What are you doing here?" I whispered. I leaned against the wall, feeling dizzy, like I was about to faint. For weeks, I'd imagined to myself what I'd say if he were in front of me, and here we were. His deep blue eyes bored into mine, as if he was searching for something.

"I'm here with . . . never mind that, why have you cut me out of your life? I thought we were friends." He frowned at me as my mouth gaped open. *He* thought we were friends? I pushed past him as the tears began to sting. I wasn't going to cry. Not here.

"Beth, wait!" His voice echoed down the hall, a sense of urgency noticeable in his tone. I rounded the corner back into the restaurant area and rushed toward Roman.

"Can you take me home, please?"

He nodded and stood up, taking my arm as he scanned the room. Was it that obvious that something had upset me? Thank God he didn't ask questions.

He just led me toward the exit, my hand clenched firmly in his.

"Are you okay?" he asked as I pulled my hand away.

I nodded, my fingers fiddling with the silver dress ring that donned the middle finger on my right hand. Anything to take the focus off what had just happened.

He started the car and pulled out of the parking lot. We

drove the few blocks to my place in complete silence. As we reached my front gate, I gathered my things, ready to make a quick exit.

"Beth, wait."

I jumped as his hand touched my thigh.

His brow furrowed as he studied my face. "Will you talk to me?" he asked gently.

I shook my head, and forced myself to smile. "I'm fine. I-It was just a panic attack."

He didn't look convinced, but he nodded. "Can I call you?"

"Yes."

Chapter Six

Beth

I leaned over the bathroom sink, struggling to breathe. I couldn't believe he was there. After two months, seeing him had shocked me. He'd looked good. Who was I kidding—he had looked fucking incredible. He was Coop: tall, sexy, with the deepest blue eyes. My heart ached for him.

"*Fuck.*" I lifted my head and stared at myself in the mirror. The small amount of mascara I'd put on was now streaked down my cheeks. "Why can't this just be over?" I muttered. I'd do anything to rewind to that night. I just wanted the old me back, only I didn't know how to do that.

The intercom rang. I splashed cold water on my face, patting it dry with a hand towel. I still looked like a mess, but not nearly as bad. As I approached the intercom, I wondered who it could be. Did I want it to be Coop?

Yes…No…I felt so confused.

"Yes?"

"Beth, it's Roman. Can you buzz me in?"

I pressed the button, wondering what he wanted. I paced by the door while I waited for him to knock. When he did, I opened the door, leaning against it.

"I'm sorry, but I can't leave you like this. Something is obviously wrong. Look at you, you're shaking."

"I'm fine," I stammered, my heart pounding. I was both shocked and touched by his concern.

"You don't look fine. Call me overprotective, but I cannot leave you like this. Either you let me inside or I'm sleeping on your porch for tonight." He glanced around, folding his arms across his chest. I scowled at him. "Pretty cold out here already." It was barely two in the afternoon and the sun was still out.

"Fine." I let the door swing open.

He flashed me a smile and walked inside, shutting the door behind him. "I knew you wouldn't let me freeze."

I rolled my eyes and motioned for him to follow me.

"I was just about to make some lunch, if you want some." Cringing, I thought about Coop and having to race out of the restaurant.

"Sounds good. But you sit down and let me make something. Please?" he added when I opened my mouth to protest.

I sighed. It would be easier just to give in and let him help. It was obviously the only way to get rid of him. "Fine," I sighed.

He busied himself in the kitchen as I sat at the table, my head resting in my hands. My mind was still on Coop. Seeing him had been such a shock. He'd looked good.

"Do you actually have any food?"

I glanced up. Roman was leaning against the kitchen counter. He looked amused. Shit. I still hadn't gone shopping.

"I'm really not that hungry anyway," I replied.

"You have to eat, Beth. Let me order a pizza."

"Okay," I agreed.

He pulled out his phone. "What do you like?"

"Whatever," I muttered. Right then, I couldn't care less about what toppings were on my pizza.

After he'd ordered, he convinced me to join him in the living room. I followed him in there, sinking down into one of the black leather recliners. Roman picked up the remote and turned on the TV.

"Seinfeld?" he asked. I shrugged, resting my head on the armrest. He sat down and quickly became engrossed in the sitcom. I loved that he didn't try to force conversation on me. The last thing I felt like doing at the moment was talking. We watched the TV until lunch arrived, then continued to watch it while we ate. I managed about half a slice of pizza.

"I might go to bed," I said, pushing my plate over onto

the coffee table. "I think what I need is a good night's sleep."

He studied me for a moment and then nodded.

"You can go if you like. I promise I'm fine."

"Okay. I'll leave you alone. But promise me you'll call if you need anything?"

I nodded. I stood up and walked him to the door.

"Sweet dreams, beautiful." He kissed me on the nose. I locked the door after him and trudged down to my bedroom.

Stripping my clothes off, I climbed into my huge empty bed, pulling the covers up tightly around my neck. I hoped what I was feeling could be cured by sleep. But somehow I doubted it.

Chapter Seven

Roman

Arriving home, my mind was still on Beth and this afternoon at lunch. One minute she had been happy and laughing, and the next she was in the midst of a panic attack. The urgency in her voice when she'd come back from the bathroom had scared me. My first thought was that she'd been attacked or confronted by someone, but then she kept assuring me she was okay . . . now I didn't know what to believe.

Throwing my keys on the kitchen counter, I grabbed a can of soda and went straight into my study, kicking the door shut with my foot. I shrugged my jacket off and hung it on the back of the door, and then I sank into my chair. Sighing, I reached up and curled my fingers around my tie, yanking it loose and throwing it onto the desk.

Fuck. I ran my hands through my short hair, lacing my fingers together behind my head. I closed my eyes and tried to remember how important this job was to me—how important it was for me to get paid. And then I thought about her.

Beth.

I knew more about Beth than she probably knew about herself: a side effect of my job. I knew she'd started her singing career when she was fifteen. I knew she had no family, that her mother had died when she was twelve, and that her father had left when she was two. I knew she had been cared for, for most of her life, by her sister—if you could call it caring. She had been through so much shit, I got angry just thinking about it.

I knew every little detail that had ever been written about her, things in her history that even she didn't realize. I felt as if I'd known her all my life.

Even with the little connection we had, I felt bad about what I was doing. We were forming a friendship, one based on lies. This girl had been through so much hurt, and here I was adding to that.

There had been nothing in my contract about befriending her. That was all on me. *Watch and report* was what I'd been told. That was what I was being paid to do.

"What the fuck are you doing, Hale?" I muttered, flicking a rouge rubber band off the desk. I watched as it flew across the room, landing just short of the door.

No matter how much I told myself that everything was fine, I knew somehow I was going to fuck this up. I always did. It was like my trademark. I had more secrets buried under my layers than the fucking Playboy Mansion. Nothing was what it seemed when it came to me, and things always seemed to backfire at the worst times.

My whole life depended on this going according to plan. If I fucked this up, I could kiss the club goodbye, and probably several of my fingers. Carlos didn't mess around.

I could do this. I could keep my distance and not do anything stupid. I laughed loudly, knowing already that there was no way in hell I was going to sit back and do nothing. I had to figure this girl out.

Cursing, I reached for a glass and sloshed it half full of whisky, single malt and aged—only the best for me. Everything about me oozed money, but I knew better than anyone that looks could be deceiving. There had been a time when I'd been that person: a man who had everything he could ever want for. That felt like a lifetime ago. I sighed as I drank the entire contents of the glass in one mouthful.

A few years ago, I had been that guy. The one everyone wanted to be. The guy with more than a few hundred dollars in his bank account—but all that had changed. And that was the thing I had to remember: things could change so quickly, with no warning. One minute you're happy and carefree, and the next your whole world is falling apart around you.

A soft rap on the door got my attention. I looked up and saw Scarlett standing there, a mug in her hand.

"I thought you could use a coffee."

"Thanks," I sighed. She walked in, placing the mug in front of me, then stood awkwardly by the desk. "You can sit down." I chuckled. She flushed, and practically fell into the large leather recliner. I had to stop myself from laughing. Scarlett oozed confidence, especially at the club, but when we were alone at home, all that changed. She became a different person.

"Are you scared of me, Scarlett?" I asked, amused.

Her eyes widened as her pretty little mouth fell open. "No," she replied indignantly. "It's just . . . well, I never know what mood I'm going to catch you in. Y-you've changed since . . . well, since it happened." She quickly glanced away as my face darkened.

Ah, yes, the incident. At least, that was what the police called it. I knew better, though. I knew that had it not been for my actions, Louisa would still be here. Now only God knew where she was.

It had been three years, six months, and four days since that day—the day I changed into the man sitting here, drowning his sorrows in a bottle of scotch worth more than he had in his bank account.

Beautiful and young, Scarlett had been my assistant

for the last three years. She was my right-hand girl who handled most of the frontline promotion for the club. I much preferred to run things from behind the scenes.

Scarlett possessed many of the traits I looked for in a partner: she had a willingness to learn, and an eagerness about her that excited me. She was like a lost little puppy, desperate for praise from her master. Whatever I asked, she'd do it—even seducing drunken pop stars.

Between the odd hours of the club and my need for companionship, it seemed logical for Scarlett to live with me. She doubled as my housemaid, preparing meals and doing light cleaning in exchange for lodging. It had suited her at the time, freshly evicted and looking for somewhere to live. Slowly, we had become used to our arrangement.

I won't lie and say I hadn't thought about fucking Scarlett, because I had. Many times. But I had never stepped over that line. If there was one rule I followed religiously, it was keeping my work and private lives separate—not always easy, especially in my case. Watching her the other night in the club had been for purely professional reasons. Well, maybe not entirely professional, but it hadn't been Scarlett I'd been paying attention to.

I don't know if that made it better or worse.

"Do you still think about her?" Scarlett asked, her voice soft. Her question hit me like a brick over the head. Right away, I knew she was talking about Louisa.

"Of course I do," I replied gruffly, angry at the ridiculousness of her question. "But what happened, happened. I can't change that. God knows I paid for it. So I move on, and never make the same mistake again."

Sensing that our conversation was over, Scarlett mumbled an excuse and left the room. I sighed and tossed my empty glass at the wall, wincing as it shattered into tiny pieces. I had no idea where Louisa was, or if she was even alive. She had made no attempt to contact me, which pissed me off as much as it concerned me. She'd been seven months pregnant with our child. Didn't I at least have the right to know about him? I could accept that I'd done wrong by her, but nobody deserved to be shut out from their child's life.

***

Pushing my way out from my desk, I stood up. I was unsteady on my feet, and my stomach was woozy from the combination of lack of food and an overdose of alcohol. I stalked out of the room, slamming the door shut behind me.

"Scarlett!" I yelled, my voice echoing through the quiet house. My quiet house.

Restored to its original beauty, this was the very house I was born in, which I'd inherited once my parents had passed. My brother had no interest in keeping the place, so I'd bought his share.

I gazed over the antique staircase that wound up to the second floor. This place had class, something so many properties lacked these days. With its polished redwood floors and beautifully high ceilings, you couldn't help but marvel at the design and the intricate details of the hand-carved cornices and delicate architrave.

I glanced down the hall as Scarlett came running, her bare feet softly thumping against the floor. Her long blonde hair was twisted into a bun, and she wore a short floral sundress that highlighted her long, slim legs.

"Yes?" she said, her breathing labored. My neck

stiffened, the burst of color in her cheeks stirring something inside of me. Arousal. I pushed it away and kept my expression emotionless.

"I'll be out for the next few hours. Please redirect any calls to my cell." She nodded and retreated back into the kitchen. I watched her go, my eyes lingering on her ass. "Oh, and Scarlett?" She turned, waiting for me to speak. "I dropped a glass in my study. That will need cleaning up."

***

I headed outside, pulling on my jacket as I walked to the car. It was a clear, sunny day, but the morning frost was just present enough to put a chill in the air. I opened the door of my Porsche 911 and slid into the driver's seat, the smell of leather and grease engulfing me. God, I loved that smell. I had a passion for cars, and this baby had been my dream for many years—since I was a child. The Porsche had been the only positive thing I had taken out of my relationship with my father. That sounded harsh, but it was the truth.

Nothing had ever been good enough for him or my mother, right up until their death in a car accident six years ago. After years of fighting for their love and approval, it became easier to be the rebel of the family. I lived to break the rules. I was forever pushing boundaries, and the result was that they eventually gave up on me, saying I was a lost cause. Their love and attention was focused on my younger brother, William.

At thirty, he was two years my junior, and different from me in every way. His perfect grades and long list of extracurricular activates had paid off with a full scholarship to Boston Med. William had been the poster child for everything my parents held dear.

I hadn't seen or spoken to my brother since their funerals, and that suited me fine.

Life in the Hale household hadn't exactly been easy for me.

***

I turned the key and the engine revved to life. With a spin of the back wheels, I took off down the street, leaving a trail of smoke behind me. As I tore through the back streets with little regard for the speed limit, my mind drifted to Beth. Every time she entered my head, my heart began to pound and a layer of perspiration coated my skin. It was like thinking about her gave me a reaction.

Maybe I was allergic to cute little blonde pop stars.

What was this woman doing to me? It'd been a long time since I'd been so invested in another person's well-being. In fact, I couldn't even tell you what this was. Well, I could, but that was something I avoided thinking about whenever possible.

Fucking insane, that's what this was. If you forgot the fact that I was twelve years older than she was, and that she was pretty screwed up at the moment, then sure, maybe this could go somewhere.

Oh wait, that's right—I forgot to consider that I'd been spying on her for the last month. Because that was bound to go down well. I could just see myself working that into the conversation. Then maybe we could sit around and chuckle about the rest of the skeletons in my closet, because if she weren't scared off already, she sure as fuck would be after that.

Laughing bitterly, I swerved around the corner a little too aggressively. The car spun out of control, almost barreling into a tree. I screeched to a stop, breathing heavily.

"*Fuck.*" Maybe I needed to get laid. And most definitely not with Beth.

That's probably all this is: my hormones going crazy because a sexy young woman was paying attention to me.

I could *almost* convince myself that was true, if it weren't for the fact that pretty women threw themselves at me all the time. I had no trouble turning any of them down, so why did I find it so hard with Beth?

***

I sat in my car for a minute outside the club. I was trying so hard to rationalize what I was doing with Beth. Or what I *wanted* to do with her. I had to watch, report, and keep her safe.

That was what I was being paid to do.

I wasn't being paid to flirt with her, or fuck her, or to do anything else other than keep her out of trouble. I was supposed to keep my distance and not stir up suspicion.

She'd been out of control in the club that night. I knew the only way to get her home safely was to let her think that she was in control. The whole stunt between her and Scarlett had been my idea. It was either she went home with me or potentially end up dead in the trunk of some psycho's car. A bit dramatic maybe, but that's where she was headed.

How could this possibly end well for me? No matter where this went, if she ever found out the truth, I'd be dead.

Getting out of the car, I slammed the door shut and walked over to the back entrance. From the outside, the place looked like any of the other industrial factories that lined this part of town. Rule one of operating this kind of club: respect the patrons. They wanted to know they could come here and not end up on the front page of *Celebrity Times*. I kept my clientele small, and so far I'd managed to avoid any major confidentiality breaches.

Unlocking the door, I walked inside and disabled the alarm. Inside, everything was pure luxury: the main bar area was fitted with state-of-the-art modern furnishings, plush sofas and Italian marble surfaces. We were fully booked each and every night. This wasn't the type of establishment you could just turn up at and expect entry. Bookings were made months in advance, with only a handful of patrons extended the privilege of regular entry. Those were our VIP clients, and more often than not, silent investors.

My entire savings had gone into this place, and a nice little wad of money I didn't have. Getting involved with Carlos Petrotrov might not have been the safest move, but it had been the only one I had available. I'd needed the cash so they'd supplied it when the banks wouldn't touch me. Apparently, a juvenile record will upset a lot of things in life. But I had the cash, and the means to repay the loan. How could things go wrong?

The answer was *very fucking easily*.

My office was located down the back, away from the main bar. I flicked on the lights in the office and grabbed the folder of unpaid invoices I'd come down for. It had been days since I'd made an appearance, and I knew I'd need to put one in soon. Many of the members came here expecting to see me. Not only that, but I enjoyed it—not as the owner, but as a participant.

I also liked the staff to know I was around, and that I had control of things. Because a place like this could so easily spiral out of hand. I had a good team, but that didn't mean mistakes couldn't be made—or that they hadn't been made before.

My mind briefly wandered back to Louisa. Sweet Louisa. *Fuck!* They say everything happens for a reason, but I lost faith in a lot of things that day. Louisa had been special, and then she was gone.

There had been something about her that had drawn me in from the first day we met. It wasn't love at first sight—because who really believes in that shit?—but she had definitely stopped me in my tracks, with her long dark hair and sad blue eyes. I reached up and wiped the film of sweat that had formed on my brow, and unclenched my fists.

If there was one thing I'd learned the hard way, it was always maintain the illusion of power, even if inside you feel as helpless as shit.

Chapter Eight

Beth

Putting the incident with Roman out of my mind was actually much harder than I'd thought it would be. After an afternoon of going to the gym, I was waiting for a doctor's appointment when I finally broke down and texted him. I wasn't used to guys backing off from me the way he had.

So, am I going to be seeing you again?

My phone buzzed a few minutes later. Smiling, I pressed answer without checking whom the call was from. Rookie mistake.

"Beth?"

Shit. Fuck. Coop.

My heart dropped. I had no idea what to say. I stopped, and I nearly fell off my chair. My heart was beating furiously, as if it were about to break out of my chest.

Hearing his voice brought back all of the emotions from that night. I couldn't do this. I couldn't speak to him. Running into him the other day had been hell.

"Coop." It didn't even sound like me. Scratchy and about five notes too high, my voice sounded like a squirrel being strangled. I took a deep breath and rubbed the back of my neck as the woman two seats down gave me a sideways glance.

"Why the fuck have you been ignoring me, Beth? I've been texting, calling. And then the other day . . ." He stopped, as if he was having trouble believing I'd actually answered. "What the hell is wrong? Let me come over."

"Oh, are you sure your little girlfriend won't mind?" I asked bitterly. "I can't see you, Coop. I can't explain, but I just need space. Can you give me that?"

"I'll give you all the space you need once I'm sure you're okay." Fuck. He sure was persistent.

I sighed, wondering what it was going to take to get him off my back. I couldn't cope with this. Not right now. Thinking about him made me think about what had happened, and I'd worked too hard to block that out to fall apart now.

"I'll email you." *Email? What was I, in high school?*

"Email?" he said dubiously, echoing my thoughts.

"Yes. Email. I can't put this all into words—it's too embarrassing, okay?" The only way to get the space I needed from him was to admit half of the truth, and I was fucked if I was going to do that over the phone in the middle of a packed doctor's office.

"Fine. But if this doesn't happen today, I swear I'm going to start showing up in public. I'm worried about you." His tone was serious. And he would do that, too. In fact, it surprised me that he hadn't already.

"I'll do it today, okay? Bye." I quickly hung up, and saw a message waiting from Roman.

Are you asking me out?

I bit my lip to fight a smile as I replied.

No. I have no interest in pursuing anything with you.

He replied right away.

Then why are you texting me?

I laughed out loud. He had a point. Maybe . . .

Beth, forget it! You are not ready for anything. You can barely handle friendship at the moment.

Sorry, Roman, I'm not buying the I-want-you-but-I-don't-want-you routine. It's getting old pretty quickly. This is purely platonic.

I fidgeted nervously, waiting impatiently for him to reply.

If I seem odd, it's because I don't want to ruin this friendship that I may or may not be starting with a beautiful woman much younger than me. I just don't want to fuck you up, Beth. Believe it or not, I'm not that type of guy.

I sat there rereading the message until I was called into

the exam room. I stood up and followed the doctor into the room, my head racing.

As if he could fuck me up any more than I already am.

A familiar feeling washed over me, one I couldn't quite put my finger on. Then I realized what it was that I was feeling: *happy*. For the first time since the assault, I was happy.

Still, I wasn't sure that I could just be friends with Roman. My track record with guys as friends wasn't exactly stellar. I quickly texted a reply and then shoved my phone in my pocket.

Roman, you're a nice guy, but I don't think I'm ready for anything . . . not even friendship.

"Ms. Masters. How can I help you today?"

Dr. Novak squinted at me over the rim of his glasses, his kind eyes immediately putting me at ease. He had been my doctor for the past four years. He was somebody I trusted—someone I knew was always there to help me.

"I'm having trouble sleeping," I explained, pushing

my hair back into place behind my ear. I hadn't seen a doctor since that night at the hospital. Had they sent the records to him? Why hadn't I given a false name or something?

"Is there anything in particular bothering you, Beth?"

I shrugged. "Work, mostly. I have a lot of deadlines at the moment and I'm struggling to shut my brain off at night." It wasn't a complete lie.

His bushy gray eyebrows creased together. He glanced at his laptop, then back at me. "Beth, I want to talk to you about the night at the hospital." *Oh no.* "You had bruising consistent with a sexual assault. Have you spoken to anyone about it?"

I thought about denying it, but I was just so sick of everything. I sighed, deflated. What good would talking to someone about it now do? It happened so long ago.

"No. But I'm fine, I promise." My words came out like a plea. I wouldn't believe I was fine, and I doubted he would either.

"Beth." He paused and pursed his lips. "I understand

you not wanting to report it, but would you at least consider counseling? There are many good services out there, especially for women in your position."

"Thanks, I appreciate your help, but I'm fine. Honestly."

He stared hard at me for a moment. I stared back. Could he see through my act? All I wanted was something to help me sleep and I'd be fine.

He scribbled out my prescription and handed it to me. He also pushed a brochure across the desk. I took both. *Sexual Assault.* I sighed.

"Just think about it. Please," he asked earnestly.

I nodded. If it would shut him up, then I'd take the damn brochure. I stood up and shoved them both in my bag.

"See you soon, Beth."

I left the doctor's and immediately checked my phone for a reply from Roman. I sighed. Nothing. My mood dulled even further when I remembered my promise to Coop. Great. Now, I had to compose the world's most awkward email.

Shit.

***

Dragging open my laptop, I double clicked on the email icon. I tapped my fingers on the table, not sure how to start what I needed to say. All the words were in my head, it was just hard putting them down in a way that wouldn't make me sound like I was crazy.

Just write down everything you feel. You can edit it before you hit send.

Coop,

The truth is, I'm in love with you. Or I was— maybe I still am. Seeing you happy, as much as I want that for you, breaks my heart because it wasn't me you chose. I know you probably had no idea how I felt, but can you understand how much of an idiot I felt like,

falling for the guy I was paying to have sex with me?

I'll get over it, but it's going to take me time. I hope you can understand that's why seeing you is not possible right now, and I really hope you can respect that.

Always,

Beth.

I hit send without a second thought. I didn't want to sit there dwelling over the past. The only way for me to get over him, and what had happened, was to push them both out of my mind.

I'd just reached a new high of embarrassment: telling my former male prostitute that I'd been in love with him for the last eight months.

Chapter Nine

Roman

I poured myself a glass of whisky over ice and shrugged out of my jacket, hanging it neatly over the back of the chair. My phone beeped. I read the message and raised my eyebrows.

The Carousel tonight. Well, that was something different. Again, Beth was surprising me. The Carousel was definitely a popular haunt for celebrities, but a little more sophisticated than the type of place I'd have expected her to go for. I replied to my contact and headed for the bathroom, leaving the untouched drink sitting on the counter.

"Scarlett?" I hollered, walking down the hallway. Silence greeted me. Satisfied that I was alone, I headed into the bathroom. I unbuttoned my shirt and peeled it off, disposing of it in the laundry hamper. I unzipped my pants, and stepping out of them and my boxers, I walked over to the shower and turned it on. The steam from the hot water rose quickly toward the ceiling vent, filling the bathroom.

God, that feels good.

Nothing matched the feeling of a nice hot shower, especially on a cold day. Tilting my head back, I sighed as the water drizzled over my face, plastering my hair against my forehead.

Pouring the liquid soap into the palm of my hand, I massaged it into my skin, paying extra attention to my cock, which hardened against my touch. My mind wandered back to Beth and Scarlett last week—how badly I'd just wanted to rip out my dick and jerk off. Beth had me feeling so fucking turned on that it had taken all my resolve to stay in control. And then in her kitchen, when she took off that robe, with her perfect round breasts, and her hard, erect nipples pointing at me, begging to be sucked . . .

Fuck, I want her so badly it hurts.

I curled my hand around my erection and closed my eyes, picturing that perfect little body. God, the things I

wanted to do to her. I thought about the club—my club—
and imagined taking her there. How would she react? She
struck me as the kind of girl who would enjoy it, but with
her I just couldn't quite tell if all that promiscuity was just
an act.

But that didn't stop me from imagining she was
kneeling in front of me, taking my cock in her tight little
mouth. I groaned, picturing those big green eyes gazing up
at me as she sucked furiously. My fist worked the length of
my shaft with speed as the pressure began to build inside
me.

"Fuck," I hissed as I ejaculated, the pounding water
washing away all the evidence. Leaning my head against
the tiled wall, I breathed heavily, trying to regain my
composure and refusing to feel guilty about what I'd just
done. If it prevented me from doing something stupid
tonight, then what harm did jerking off to her do?

***

I arrived at The Carousel and paid the valet the fifteen-
dollar parking fee, even though what I really wanted to do
was park my own damn car and tell him to fuck off. Fifteen

dollars for him to move the car down three spots? What a fucking joke.

I stalked inside, still annoyed but trying to shake off my mood. Louisa used to say my ability to get worked up about silly little things was one of the things that drove her crazy.

And here I was, thinking my passion was endearing.

I never had any trouble getting in anywhere, because the right people knew who I was. Believe it or not, I had a reputation. A quiet one, but one all the same.

My club was very well known among the circles that mattered. Initially, I'd been worried that Beth would recognize me. But she didn't, thank Christ. Not that it would have changed much, but if she'd recognized me, she might have eventually connected the rest of the dots.

I spotted her, sitting by the bar, alone. Slowing to a stop, I watched her for a moment, captivated by her beauty and obvious sadness. She slowly stirred her drink with her straw, her eyes downward, oblivious to the fact that she was by far the sexiest woman in the place.

She wore a short white dress that made her tanned skin just glow, and showcased her long legs. God, she was doing to me what no other woman had been able to do in years. She was making me feel something. I could call it feeling sorry for her all I wanted, but the reality was that every single time I saw her I had to fight the urge to throw her down and fuck her until she could barely walk.

Get it together and remember what you're being paid to do. I knew exactly what was on the line here, and I was stupid if I was willing to throw all that away for some woman I barely even knew.

Chapter Ten

Beth

Another evening spent in a random club trying to forget my problems. Well, maybe not so random. This was one of the most exclusive clubs in the area. They didn't just let anyone in. I glanced to my left, where Miley Cyrus was taking body shots off the chest of a busty blonde. Well, maybe they'd relaxed their standards a little.

The funny thing was, every morning began the same.

I was going to change.

I was in a funk, and I was going to fix it. I wasn't going to let myself get out of control. I could have all the motivation in the world and then somehow end up back here. These places were all the same: the same people and the same problems.

Nothing *ever* changed.

"Well, fancy seeing you here."

I turned around and found myself staring into the dark eyes of Roman. His lip curled upward as he took in my expression, his gaze then traveling down my body appreciatively. I felt my nipples harden under the scrap of sheer white chiffon that was my dress, my body reacting to his intense stare.

"What are you doing here?" I asked, raising an eyebrow.

The racing heart, the tingles, the blank mind—it was all there, just like every other time I saw him. I felt like a little kid around him. He intimidated me. I was used to being such a confident person, but the attack had reduced me to an insecure, self-obsessed mess. He made me feel safe, but out of my comfort zone. With him I felt alive and not just like I was going through the motions. If anyone could bring the old me back, it was him.

There was a big part of me that was excited to see him.

As honest as I was being in the text that I'd sent him, deep down I didn't want him to take no for an answer. Just like I didn't want Coop giving up on me.

"Oh, you own the place now, do you?" he chuckled. I was having trouble staying on my seat. I told myself it was the three vodkas I'd had, but looking into those damn sexy eyes, I couldn't be sure it wasn't him.

He slid into the tiny space between me and the bar counter, between my legs, his thighs pressing against mine.

Oh. My. God.

My eyes were level with his chest, and I was staring at the outline of his ripped muscles through his fitted shirt. I raised my head, my eyes meeting his, embarrassed by how he made me feel.

"You okay there, Beth?" he murmured, his eyes laughing at me.

Was I okay?

No. I wasn't. I had an insanely sexy older man pressed so close against me I was sure he could feel the heat bursting from between my legs. God, what he did to me . . . Or rather, what I *wished* he'd do to me. I threw back the last of my drink.

"I doubt it would make a difference if I did own the place," I retorted smugly, forcing our conversation back on track. "What do you want from me, Roman? I'm too tired to play your games tonight." I rubbed my temples, trying to will away the pressure building behind my eyes.

"Hey, I'm just a guy out on the town. It's not my fault we both have very expensive tastes." Ah, why was he looking at me like that? And why was my body reacting this way? "We're very similar, you and I," he continued, his fingers stroking the top of my leg. "We're both used to getting what we want."

"And yet we don't seem to want the same things," I retorted, annoyed. "Make yourself useful and buy me a drink."

He narrowed his eyes at me and smiled, reaching for my glass. I held my breath as he moved slowly past me and down to the other end of the bar. As soon as he was gone, I heaved a sigh of relief.

What was it with this guy? Everything about him affected me, and God, that attraction, it was so strong. And then I'd remember him turning me down at my house and feel sick. And embarrassed. Oh, so embarrassed.

What the fuck was so wrong with me that I had no luck whatsoever with men? Sure, I could find plenty of guys who'd love to fuck me, but a relationship? It was like I was doomed.

Roman was back soon, a vodka-and-cranberry and a glass of straight whiskey balanced in one hand. He remembered what I like. I fought to keep a grin from taking over my lips.

Calm down, Beth. So he remembered what you like to drink. Not a big deal.

"Thanks," I mumbled, taking it from him.

He smiled and took the vacant seat next to me.

"So, it's a total coincidence seeing you here, huh?" I didn't know why, but I felt suspicious. There were a million bars around here he could've gone to, and he happened to walk into mine?

"Guess so." He raised an eyebrow as he took a sip of his whiskey. "You don't get sick of this?" he asked, rolling his glass between the palms of his hands.

"Sick of what?" I knew what he meant. Of course I was sick of it, but I was sick of everything. What else was I going to do? Sit at home with my imaginary friends and play charades?

"This. The partying. Being out every night."

I turned to him, a sudden rush of anger seeping through me. This guy had known me all of a week, and suddenly he was an expert on my life?

"You've met me three times, Roman. I don't think that gives you the right to make comments on my lifestyle. What business is it of yours what I do?" My voice was harsh.

He opened his mouth and then closed it. Nodding, he shrugged, his expression softening. "You're right. What you do with your life is not my problem. I'm here to drink, not to babysit."

"Babysit? I didn't ask you to be my fucking babysitter, Roman. Isn't there somewhere else you can go?" I retorted, frustrated.

He smirked at me and took a sip of his drink.

Fuck this.

I stood up and grabbed my purse. Without a glance back, I stormed out the side exit and into a deserted alleyway. Goosebumps prickled the skin on the back of my arms as I stared into the darkness. My breathing began to shallow.

"Beth, wait!"

I sighed with relief as the door opened and Roman's voice echoed through the night. I wiped under my eyes and turned around.

"Let me take you home," he offered.

I shook my head viciously. "I don't *need* you to take me home, Roman. I need you to stop messing with my head."

"I'm sorry you think that's what I'm doing, Beth," he said quietly.

Gah! Now he had me feeling bad for snapping at him. "Look, I like you, but I can't handle not knowing what the hell you want with me. One minute we're friends, then I think there could be more, then a second later I feel like I don't know you at all . . . which is funny, because I *don't*." I took a breath, calming myself down from the tangle he was working me into.

He took a step toward me. "I'd like to change that, Beth." His voice was low and gravelly.

"Why are you here, Roman? Why do you even care?" I pleaded.

"Because I see a girl who is crying out for help. This?" He waved his arms around. "This isn't you."

"You barely know me," I muttered.

He leaned over and stoked my cheek. "I know enough," he whispered.

"Fine," I grumbled, my heart melting. "Take me

home."

Chapter Eleven

Roman

She was quiet on the drive home, barely saying a word. I snuck glances at her, wondering what she was thinking. Her head rested back against the seat as she gazed out the window, lost in her own world.

My eyes wandered over her bare legs. *God, those smooth silky thighs. What I wouldn't give to be between them...*

"Watch it!" Beth screamed, clutching hold of the seat. I swerved, regaining control of the car, which had began to drift sideways toward a tree. My heart pounded as she glared at me accusingly.

"Sorry," I muttered. I wanted to add that it was her fault for being so damn sexy.

"How much did you have to drink?" she muttered, shaking her head.

"Less than you, that's for sure. Settle down, Princess, I'll get you home in one piece." I shook my head as she glared at me.

I was becoming obsessed with finding out her secrets. How did this beautiful creature harbor so much pain? She hid it well, but for someone who had known her for a long time—at least, from a distance—it wasn't hard to see.

"Where's your head?" I asked.

She jumped at the sound of my voice and turned to me. "Right here," she said, pointing upward. I rolled my eyes at her joke, but still cracked a smile. "I'm just tired." She sighed softly and went back to staring blankly into the distance. *Tired of what?* I wanted to ask. But I didn't. I was pushing her as it was. If I pushed much harder, she would shut right down on me.

***

She walked ahead of me, allowing me to admire her ass. That damn dress drove me crazy. It was so fucking short it barely covered her ass. I so badly wanted to grab hold of her and feel her up against me.

There was no denying to myself why I was going inside. I could paint it however I wanted; it wouldn't change the fact that, given the chance, I'd be fucking her senseless tonight. All I needed was a suggestion from her, a hint that she wanted it, and there would be no holding me back. That was how I did things, right? Act first and deal with the ramifications later? Why change my pattern now?

Letting the door swing open, she stood back to let me through first. I smiled at her, then walked inside.

She flicked the light switch, and the hallway lit up. The place was as nice as I remembered. It would have cost her a fortune. She was on the top of the hill in one of the most sought-after neighborhoods in Manhattan, overlooking the beach. Just the living area was about the size of my entire house—and my house was by no means small. The dark floorboards were perfectly polished, and the furniture looked as though it had never been used.

She headed off toward the kitchen, and I followed her, my eyes back on her ass.

"Drink?" she asked, looking over her shoulder. *Fuck.* I averted my eyes. Too late. She smirked at me.

"A coffee would be good," I mumbled, cursing to myself.

The kitchen opened out to a large balcony that overlooked Mason's Point. At this time of night, I could just make out the outline of the surrounding hills and the scattered lights in the distance. Sliding the door open, I walked outside, the mild breeze nice against my skin.

"Here you go."

I turned to see Beth holding two mugs of coffee, steam lifting from each.

"Thanks," I said, taking one. I turned my attention back to the view. "It's really beautiful out here. It must be a great place to unwind."

She moved closer to me, until we both stood against the glass wall of the balcony. "It is," she admitted softly. "It's great place to think. I used to always sit out here and write my songs."

"Not anymore?" I asked carefully. Every other time I'd tried to have her open up she had closed off so quickly.

She shook her head and sighed. "I haven't written anything in ages," she said. God, I wished I could take away that fear in her voice. What had her so damn afraid? "It's like my creativity stopped when—" She stopped abruptly and wandered back over to the lounge chairs.

"When what?" I pressed, sitting down beside her.

She flushed. "Nothing." I watched her as she set her mug down on the concrete floor. She sat on the lounge chair, knees bent, one leg on either side, her bare feet on the ground. I hadn't even realized she'd taken off her shoes.

Setting my own drink down, I stood up and sat down on her chair, facing her. Her eyes widened as she wondered what I was doing. She laughed as I reached for her foot, planting it in front of me.

"God, yes," she mumbled, throwing her head back as I gently began to rub. "Oh hell, that feels good."

"Do you like what you do?" I asked as my fingers worked the kinks in her foot.

"I don't know," she said honestly. "I'm smart enough to understand that I need to make a living. How many people actually enjoy what they do?" She shrugged, as if she had nothing else to say.

"I think people who are unhappy in their chosen career use that as an excuse not to move on."

"Maybe," she agreed, "but what else am I going to do? This is all I've been for five years. Before that, I was just a kid. Besides, I'm independent. I don't have to worry about money, and I've got a lifestyle most people only dream of."

"You're also lonely and unhappy."

"Really?" she said, cocking her head. "And tell me, Mr. Big Shot, what do you propose I do? Quit my job and knit sweaters for cats?"

"Do you have a cat?" I asked, running my hand over her calf. I couldn't remember seeing one.

"No," she grumbled. "I'm allergic." I laughed and continued to let my fingers explore her smooth skin, going

as high as her thighs before running back down her legs.
"That feels . . . really fucking good." She breathed out, a
little moan escaping from her lips.

Fuck, she was so sexy. She had no idea what she was
doing to me right then with her hair all messed up, wearing
that fucking tiny dress. I swallowed hard, my eyes on her
stiff nipples, which I could make out through her dress.

Swinging her armchair around until she was facing me, I
continued to rub her feet, working my hands along her
arches. I watched her lie before me, every so often biting
her lip, and I struggled to focus. The way her dress was
creeping up and exposing her tanned skin was making me
hard.

She stretched out her toes, her heel digging into my
crotch. A smile crept onto my lips as her eyes fluttered
open and met mine when her foot made contact with my
hard cock.

"What?" I asked her.

She shrugged, pulling her foot away, tucking it under
her. "Nothing," she blushed.

"You're incredibly sexy, Beth. Of course touching you is going to arouse me."

"If touching my feet excites you, I can only imagine what touching other parts of me would do to you." She stood up and stepped over my legs until she was kneeling over me. I glanced up at her, my hand positioned on her thigh. She smiled, a contradiction to the pain hiding in her eyes. I studied her for a moment, my brow creasing as I tried to figure her out.

But it was impossible. *She* was impossible. And drunk. Not so drunk that she had no control over her behavior, but definitely drunk enough to mask whatever it was she was trying to block out.

My jaw tensed as her body fell against mine, that sexy blonde hair falling around her face. I reached up and tucked some loose strands behind her ear where they stayed momentarily before escaping again, cascading around her eyes. She smiled as she brought her mouth down onto mine, her lips feeling electric against me.

I kissed her back. No matter how badly I wanted to push her away, I wanted her more. Was I an asshole for doing this? She was drunk and I was not, but holy fuck, all I could think about was being inside of her.

I sat up, my arm curving around the arch of her back as we continued to kiss, our mouths melting into each other. I tasted her as my tongue massaged hers. She cried out, laughing, as I flipped her onto her back, positioning myself over her. I stared down at the beautiful sight before me.

She was fucking amazing. Starting at the top of her foot, my fingers ran over her soft skin. She gasped as they reached her thighs, which were exposed by her dress. I eased myself between her legs, my erection pressed urgently against the constriction of my pants.

I groaned as she lowered my zipper and reached inside my boxers. Her fingers closed around my girth as I attempted to shrug off my pants. Sounds escaped from me as she ran her fingers up and down my cock.

I watched as she reached for her dress, slipping it over her head and letting it fall over her breasts, then her stomach, before finally slipping off her hips. A familiar aching began to stir in my groin. I wanted her so fucking bad. Nothing would've satisfied me more than spreading her over that kitchen counter inside and taking her. I wanted to make her feel things she'd never felt before. I wanted to make her scream, I wanted to make her orgasm over and over until she couldn't handle it.

She knelt down in front of me, one hand resting on my chest, the other hand curled around the base of my cock. Holy fuck, what was she doing to me? She took me in her mouth, her tongue running along the base of my shaft. Fuck, this girl knew what she was doing. I ran my hands through her hair, latching onto a handful as I pushed myself further inside her mouth.

"God, yeah." I moved further down the lounge chair so I could spread my legs further apart, giving her better access. I glanced down, my eyes on her as she worked those sweet, soft lips up and down. Watching her was just as much of a turn-on as feeling her.

I was so hard now. I could feel the blood pulsating through my cock. But I wanted more. I wanted to feel inside her. I wanted to come while her pussy tightened around my cock, milking the orgasm out of me.

"Come here," I demanded, pulling her towards me. She did as I asked, straddling me as I pushed her dress up and out of the way. She wore a skimpy white thong. Thrusting it out of the way, I began to stroke her, teasing her. Arching her back, she cried out as I rubbed her stiff nipples between my fingers. Sliding my finger inside of her, I could feel her wetness. She was so damn hot, and so ready for me. Reaching into the pocket of my jeans to retrieve a condom, I quickly rolled it on.

With my hands on her hips, I lifted her onto me. My jaw clenched as I slid inside her tight wet pussy. She moaned as my hands traveled up to her breasts. I squeezed them gently, rolling her nipples between my fingers as she rode my cock. She leaned back, placing her arms on my thighs as I thrust inside of her.

"You're so wet," I mumbled. I placed my hands on her hips and bounced her toward me, driving my length into her as far as I could. She clenched her legs beside me, her pussy gripping onto my cock as I moved inside of her.

"Yes, fuck yes," she sighed, closing her eyes.

From my viewpoint, the sight of her spread back on top of me, my cock driving into her, was fucking incredible. I could feel the pressure building inside me, heightening with every movement.

"Oh god, I'm going to...I'm about to..." She gasped as I

slid a finger in, alongside my cock, circling her sweet spot.

She screamed, her back arching as I pumped into her, harder and faster, my own load on the verge of exploding. She slowed, riding me, enjoying the aftermath of her climax. My grip on her hips tightened as I came, releasing inside of her.

Sighing, she collapsed onto my stomach. My fingers stroked her back, her skin cold and clammy, a thin film of sweat covering us both.

I smiled as she stood up, pulling her dress down to cover herself. And then I noticed her expression. Where I felt mind-blown by an amazing experience with a hot, sexy, beautiful woman, she looked sad. Almost upset.

"Are you okay?" I sat up, pulling up my jeans and buttoning them. She nodded, taking a step back as I took a step towards her. "You don't seem okay. What's wrong?" I was beginning to doubt my abilities. I'd never had any complaints before, but she looked like she was moments from bursting into tears.

"Was I that bad?" It was a joke. A bad one, but I was just trying to lighten the mood. Luckily, she cracked a smile. The smile turned into a laugh. She sat down on the lounge chair opposite me and shook her head.

"You were wonderful," she said shyly. "I'm sorry, I just… The alcohol… I'm just feeling a bit off, that's all."

"Can I do anything? Do you want a glass of water? Or maybe a heat pack?" I was really worried about her. This wasn't a normal post-sex reaction.

She shook her head. "I think I just need a decent sleep. I'm sure I'll be better in the morning." She hesitated before continuing. "This is going to sound really rude, but would you mind going?"

I began to laugh. I couldn't help it. It was just the idea of being kicked out by woman after sex. She covered her face with her hands.

"I'm sorry," she said, clearly embarrassed.

"Beth, it's fine. Get a good night's rest. I'll give you a call tomorrow, okay?"

She nodded and smiled. We walked together to the front door.

"Do you mind if I kiss you?" I thought I'd better ask her permission.

She laughed and wrapped her hands around my neck. I took that as an invitation. My thumb gently stroked her cheek as I lifted her mouth to mine. We kissed slowly, my tongue dipping into her mouth, tasting her sweetness.

I could do this all night. Well, I could have if she wasn't kicking me out.

"Thanks for being so understanding," she mumbled, dropping her arms away from me.

I winked at her and gave her one more kiss on the forehead. "Get some sleep, beautiful. Call me if you need anything?" I asked. She nodded.

Chapter Twelve

Beth

I opened the fridge and surveyed the contents. As usual, the selection was minimal: some low-fat cheese, an apple that looked as though it had been sitting there for weeks, and a tub of what looked like leftover curry, which I couldn't recall ordering.

Obviously, I needed to go shopping. Maybe I could send Noni. Shopping for shoes was one thing, but I couldn't stand shopping for food. Grabbing the notepad from the kitchen counter, I began to write a list.

When I was done, I glanced back over it. *God, my personal trainer would have a heart attack if he saw some of the junk on here.*

Yes, I had a personal trainer, because I fucking hated to exercise; unless there was someone there to force me to do it, it would never get done. Not that I'd been to see him much over the past two months. Last week was the first session I'd had in ages.

Sighing, I opened the cupboard and located my emergency crackers. Well, they were now three months past the best-before date, but who was I to be picky? I carried them and a glass of water over to my desk. Just as I sat down, my email beeped. I clicked open.

Coop. Shit, shit, shit.

I hadn't heard from him since my confession the week before. My heart pounded as I clicked on the message. I waited impatiently as it loaded, both dreading and excited about reading his response. What the hell could he say to the email I'd sent him? I was about to find out.

Beth,

Firstly, wow. Holy shit, I had no idea you felt that way, and now I feel like a first-class asshole for some of the things I said to you. What I don't get is why you were pushing me into this relationship with Mia if you

felt this way.

I get that seeing me with her would be hard for you, but I really don't want to lose our friendship. If you need space, I'll give you that, but I really need my friend right now.

Love you,

Coop.

Tears rolled down my cheeks as I read the email for the tenth time. He missed me, and I missed him. Maybe avoiding him wasn't the answer. Maybe pushing him away was what was keeping me from moving on? If I pushed him away, then I had someone to blame for what had happened. Letting Coop back into my life meant actually dealing with what had happened to me rather than avoiding it.

I wasn't sure I was ready for that yet, just like I wasn't sure I was ready to let someone new into my heart.

Roman.

My heart sank. After the previous night, I wasn't sure

if I was ever going to see him again. I wouldn't blame him if he avoided me. What the hell had I been doing? The truth was, since the attack, every time I'd been intimate with someone I'd been so full of alcohol that I really had no idea what was going on.

Turning off the computer, I stood up. I needed to think about this, about Coop. His words drove through me, over and over. He wanted his friend back. The thing was, so did I. More than anything, I wanted things to be like they were.

Until late into the evening, I lay curled up on the sofa, clutching a cushion to my stomach while I watched an old black-and-white movie.

I could ignore only the constant ringing of my phone for so long. After ten minutes of nonstop ringing, I got up and went to retrieve it. That's what I got for leaving it in the kitchen. On loud.

"What?" I muttered, picking it up without checking the number.

"Beth." Ivan. I sighed. *Well, that's what I get for not*

checking the number. There was a reason for caller ID, so why didn't I ever fucking use it?

"Yes, Ivan, what do you want?" My skin prickled at the sound of his voice. Just the thought of him made my stomach turn. I tried to focus on my breathing, but I was already feeling dizzy and lightheaded.

"Now, that's no way to speak to your manager, is it?" he drawled. "Listen, I've lined you up for a movie audition. Six months in L.A. Shooting starts in three months, the girl they had lined up broke her neck. I'm sending the script over now. Take a look, and we'll talk."

"Fine. Whatever." I shuddered. Ivan's definition of "talk" differed from that of most people. I'd learned that the hard way.

"You just remember who got you where you are, honey. You might want to drop the attitude," he warned.

I hung up the call. If I kept on the line, I'd say something I'd regret. I knew I would. It was only a matter of time before I blew up at him, and to be honest, that scared the hell out of me. Pushing the devil's buttons was not a good way to stay out of trouble.

***

A courier dropped off the script a few hours later. I'd never done a movie. I'd never acted before at all, beyond my music videos.

Acting hadn't really been something that interested me, but maybe getting out of New York was a good thing. Especially if it meant getting away from Ivan.

I read through the summary of the movie, and the role I was auditioning for. It was about a girl who leaves her small town for L.A. to make her dreams of becoming a singer come true.

Sounded like the back story of every wannabe in L.A.—myself included. That was me, five years ago. Only I'd been "lucky" enough to meet Ivan.

I flipped through the script, trying to decide whether this was something I actually wanted to do. I sang because I had a good voice, and honestly, it was just luck that I'd taken off the way that I had. If I stopped singing today, I wouldn't miss it. It was something I did because I knew nothing else, and it made me enough money to be self-reliant. But not everything was about money. Hell, I was barely twenty, yet some days I felt so old and worn, like my life was nearly over.

I need to get out of here.

Tossing the script aside, I went to the bedroom and swung open my closet. I had enough outfits to go a year without wearing the same thing, and all were designer. I picked out a coral dress that cinched at the waist, and paired it with some black sandals. I knew exactly where I was headed, and why I was headed there.

***

Digging through my purse, I found my vibrating phone, checking the ID this time before answering. My pulse quickened. It was him.

"Hey," I said, trying to sound casual. "What's up?"

"Not much," Roman chuckled. "What are you up to? Are you out? I hear music."

"I'm at The Carousel." I held my head high, not giving away for a second that I'd been hoping to run into him. *Or the fact that my ass has been parked on this barstool for the past hour because of it.*

"Oh, really?" he mused. "Waiting for someone?"

I face-palmed. His voice had that tone to it, one that clearly said *I know exactly why you're there.*

"No. Just having a drink with some friends," I retorted. Friends? Sure, me and my army of imaginary buddies were kicking things up. Could I be any more pathetic?

"Well, good for you. But Beth?"

"What?"

"Don't party too hard." He chuckled.

"Yeah, thanks," I said, narrowing my eyes. I had no intention of partying too hard tonight. Or at least I hadn't, until he'd suddenly shown an interest. "See you later, Roman." I hung up before he could respond.

I looked around the bar, wondering what I was going to do now. After only a couple of drinks, my mind was still coherent enough for me to be nervous about being out in public . . . alone.

What if Ivan was here, watching me? He'd followed me once—what if he did it again? I shuddered, the thought making me want to hurl. Calling the barman over, I ordered a shot of whiskey and a vodka-and-raspberry.

"What?" I said as he raised an eyebrow. My reaction was defensive, but I couldn't help it—I was over feeling judged. He shook his head and poured my drinks, sliding them across the bar to me. Handing over the cash, I downed the shot, followed quickly by the mixer.

I slouched down into my seat, waiting for the buzz to kick in. Instead of the usual high, I found myself feeling angry, and more frustrated. I stumbled outside and waited for the cab I'd ordered a few minutes before to arrive. Why was I so angry with Roman all of a sudden? Sure, I'd been looking forward to seeing him—that was the whole reason I'd come here—but the anger was misplaced. He got under my skin, and that scared me.

He makes me feel vulnerable, and I can't handle that right now.

The cab pulled up and I climbed in, muttering my address. I stared out the window, trying to sort out what I was feeling.

"Why am I such a mess?" I mumbled to myself. Here I was lusting after a guy who I couldn't handle touching me unless I was half sloshed, but at the same time needing the rush that sex on my own terms gave me.

The driver pulled up outside my house, right next to an all too familiar black Porsche 911. Sighing, I threw a fifty at the driver and climbed out.

"Again?" I said, shutting the door of the cab. Roman smiled and walked toward me. "What do you want now?" I asked testily as I swiped the gate, still angry at the way he had gotten under my skin during our phone call.

"To see you." He came up behind me, his fingers moving my hair aside. I breathed in sharply as his lips brushed past my skin. The hairs on the back of my neck stood erect, aroused by his touch.

"What are you doing?" I mumbled, spinning around. His arms crept around my waist as he pulled me to him, his lips finding their way to mine. His lips tasted of whiskey, and I wondered how much he'd been drinking.

His lips pressed against mine as he pushed me against his car, his hands exploring my body. My head spun as his fingers ran up my thigh, looping around the skimpy fabric of my panties.

"Is this okay?" he muttered breathlessly in my ear, lifting me onto his hips as he worked my panties down.

"Yes," I whispered, kissing him as I wrapped my legs around his waist. He sat me down on the hood of his car, flinging my panties down over my knees and onto the stone driveway.

I groaned, my hands over his, guiding them under my dress and over my breasts. His fingers tweaked my nipples. Pressing his fingers against my breasts, I kissed him, hard.

Reaching down, I fiddled with the button of his pants, finally freeing his hard cock. Squeezing it, I pressed my lips against his while slowly dragging my hand up the length of his shaft.

"You've got a strong grip there," he chuckled softly. He moved onto his knees, my hold on him releasing as he pushed me down until I lay flat against the car. I sighed as his hand ran over the top of my scrunched up dress, resting on my right breast.

"Fuck…" I trembled as he rolled my nipple between his fingers.

"Part your thighs for me," he said, his other hand trailing up my inner leg. Shivers raced down my spine as I spread my legs. He kissed the inside of my thighs, leading up to the crease of my legs. I touched his hair, my fingernails exploring his scalp as he moved closer to my lips.

"*Ohh.*" My body jolted as his tongue moved swiftly along my opening. With a single finger, he held aside my lips his tongue continued to tease me. My hands gripped his hair as he thrust his tongue deep inside me, his finger massaging my sweet spot.

His talent was magical. My hold on his hair tightened, desperate to get that tongue as deep inside me as possible. At that point I didn't care if he suffocated; the only thing on my mind was the climax that was rising inside me.

"Oh yes, yes, yes!" I whispered, swinging my legs around his neck. He thrust a finger inside me while his tongue slowly licked me up and down. The combination of the two was driving me insane. "Please, oh please," I whimpered, my back arching. I reached up and fumbled with my nipples, rolling them between the tips of my fingers, the sensation pushing me over the edge.

Pleasure rippled through me. I bucked my hips into his face, needing more of him. All of him. I groaned as he danced along the fine line of ecstasy and pain, pushing him away when it all became too much.

"That was . . . wow." It was all I could manage as I straightened my dress.

He smiled at me, still leaning against the car.

"Do you want to come in?" I asked. He nodded, and followed me over to the open gate.

We walked up the path together wordlessly. What was he thinking? Because all I could think about was how amazing he had felt inside me. We reached the door. I unlocked it and let it swing open. He walked inside, with me right behind him.

"Do you, uh, want a drink?"

God, I was nervous. Why did this guy make me feel so damn nervous? Most people, I could look at their expressions and get some idea of what they were thinking. Roman? No fucking idea. He gave nothing away, and when I asked, he told me as little as possible.

Yet that hadn't stopped me from fucking a girl in front of him, or letting him take me on the hood of his car. These were things I'd never normally do, but for some reason, around him I wanted to act out. I wanted him to want me.

He followed me into the kitchen, where I found a half-empty bottle of single malt whiskey in the back of the cupboard. I hated the stuff. It tasted like ass. I opened the bottle and poised it, ready to pour into the glass when I felt his hands run up the outsides of my bare thighs. I gasped, the bottle slipping from my grasp and smashing to the floor. I didn't move. I couldn't, because his hands were now exploring between my thighs, over my damp pussy, a finger occasionally slipping inside.

Oh, God. My hands clenched on the countertop as my legs began to buckle.

"You're so wet," he whispered in my ear. "Are you

wet for me, Beth? Do you want to feel me inside you again?"

I nodded, not capable of speaking anything resembling English. All I knew was that I had an incredibly hot, mysterious, older man with his finger inside me, and I did not want him to stop.

"Oh yes," I rasped, my hips bucking toward him as he teased me.

He grabbed me by the thighs and lifted me onto the sink. I gasped, the cold metal freezing against warmth of my skin. His hands worked under my dress, the feel of his fingers against me making me tingle. I closed my eyes and lifted my arms as he slid the dress over my head. Pulling me toward him, his lips met the curve of my neck as his tongue slowly drew circles along my collarbone.

He was amazing. More than any other man I'd been with, Roman knew how to make a woman feel wanted. He pressed up against me, his lips determined to explore every inch of my body. We kissed, his tongue circling mine as his hands crept behind my back and unclipped my bra.

I sat there, naked, with him still fully dressed, and

standing between my legs. My head was hazy, but not so much that I was incapacitated. I knew what I was doing, and I wanted to be with him—the only thing was, the alcohol made that possible. Had I not been drinking, I would not be sitting on my kitchen counter naked right then, no matter who was in front of me . . . even if it were Coop.

I gasped as Roman's mouth traveled down to my breasts. His tongue circled my nipple, sucking and licking me into a state of ecstasy. I curled my legs around him as my hands ran through his hair. I kissed his forehead, breathing in the coconut-almond scent of his shampoo.

I groaned, my grip on him tightening as his fingers made their way down south. I jumped suddenly as they moved alongside my entrance. My thighs clenched with him still between them, my body aching at his touch.

"Where is your bedroom?" he asked as he gently slid a finger inside me.

"Down the hall and to the left," I whispered breathlessly. He lifted me into his arms, his kisses not slowing as he carried me toward the bedroom. I held on tightly, as if I were scared to let him go. My heart pounded. This was moving too fast. The anxiety I was beginning to feel made me worry that the effect of the alcohol was starting to wear off. When doubts started creeping into my head, I got nervous.

I couldn't do this alone. Could I?

I wanted him. God, I wanted him so badly. But in my messed up head, all I could think about right then was Ivan, and the way I had felt so useless that night.

The panic in me continued to feed on my worries. We reached the bedroom, and Roman gently lay me down on my rose embroidered bedspread, his fingers roaming all over my body.

Edging my hand inside his boxers, I gripped hold of his stiff cock, gently moving my hand back and forth. He groaned and closed his eyes, his mouth tensing as I worked my fingers up and down his shaft.

"I can't stop thinking about you," he whispered, leaning forward, his lips meeting mine. I returned the kiss with passion as his fingers continued to rub me, making me even more wet than I already was.

Still, as turned on as I was, and as much as I wanted this, I couldn't escape the past. Not today.

"Tell me how much you want me, Bethy," he whispered in my ear.

I froze. My eyes widened, and all I could feel was the pressure of him on top of me. *Bethy. Bethy.* The name shot through me like a knife.

No, no, no, no!

Frantically, I pushed him away. He was too close. I felt like the room was closing in on me, as if all the oxygen had been sucked out. I struggled to breathe. This was my first panic attack, and it was my first in the middle of sex.

I was embarrassed. I felt like a fucking fool. What the hell was wrong with me?

Swinging my legs over the edge of the bed, I sat up, wrapping the sheet around me. Roman appeared in front of me, kneeling on the floor, staring up at me with concern.

"Beth, what's wrong? Did I hurt you?"

I shook my head, the words refusing to come. I

couldn't explain this to him. What would I say? I just needed him to go. If he left, I could pull myself together and move past this, but I couldn't do it with him here, watching me.

"Please, Roman, I need you to go. I know you want answers, but right now I need to be alone."

"Are you serious? You're a mess. The hell I'm leaving you alone while you're like this. No fucking way, Beth. You don't want to talk to me? That's fine, I won't make you, but I'm not leaving until I know you're okay."

"Roman, please."

"Don't argue with me, Beth. I'll go down to the living room. Take all the time you need, and if you need to talk, I'm here for you. Don't push me away." He leaned toward me, placing a delicate kiss on my forehead. I curled up on the bed and watched as he walked out the door.

***

I sat upright in the bed, breathing hard. I must've fallen asleep. The last thing I remembered was Roman—oh my God, I didn't want to think about that right now. How could I show my face to him again? He probably thought I was a nutcase, which wouldn't be too far from the truth, but hearing that name...*Bethy.*

I reached over, grabbed two Tylenol off my bedside table, and took them with some water.

Jesus, what the hell is wrong with me?

***

Was he still here? I glanced at my phone. I'd been asleep for nearly five hours. Surely he would've left by now. Standing up, I pulled on my robe, tying it around my waist. I tiptoed down the hallway and kicked around the corner into the living room.

My heart swelled at the sight of Roman curled up on the sofa with his head resting on a cushion, fast asleep. Very quietly, I walked over to him and sat in one of the armchairs opposite. I could sit there and watch him sleep all day. As creepy as it was, that's what I felt like doing. There was no denying how protected he made me feel. Exactly what that meant, I hadn't figured out yet.

Chapter Thirteen

Roman

When I arrived at the club, I was still confused by her sudden change in mood. I hadn't been planning on going there that night, but I was getting frustrated. I needed familiarity. I needed to be able to relax, and this place was the only place that would allow me to do that.

I entered through the back and made my way down to my office, smiling at a couple of the girls on my way.

"Hello, ladies."

They smiled back, their eyes meeting before they burst into giggles. I got that reaction a lot around here. To most of these girls, I was a man with a lot of mystery about him. I kept largely to myself.

It seemed the less people knew about you, the more attractive you became. That was a big part of the allure of this club: the anonymity. People didn't come here to make friends. They weren't looking for love, or looking for a new tennis partner. They came here to play a role, to fulfill a fantasy. No questions, no expectations, and no shame.

Inside my office, I let the door shut and buzzed through to reception.

"Alli speaking."

"Hello, Alli, can you bring me a coffee please?"

"Certainly, Mr. Hale."

I hung up and then flicked on the security monitors and studied them closely. I recognized a few people—some as regulars, and some who had high profiles within the community. I knew the overweight man with the graying hair was grand jury judge Terrence Manfeld. And the slight Asian woman on the sofa with her husband was a national TV newscaster.

I watched as one of my girls engaged with them, laughing and talking before leading them into a room down

at the end of the premises. Judge Manfeld followed, taking
a seat in one of the two armchairs outside the room.

In essence, Protégé was an exclusive swingers club
with a BDSM focus. Most people associated swinging with
bad seventies hairstyles and out-of-control parties thrown
by middle-aged parents involving a bowl full of keys. That
couldn't be further from the reality I offered.

Protégé was pure class. I made sure of that.

It was a place where people could live their fantasies
of anonymous BDSM without the fear of judgment. Every
member of the club signed a non-disclosure form prior to
entry. The rules in place were there for every member's
protection, and they were non-negotiable.

I'd learned before that people who were insistent on
breaking the rules were unlikely to adhere to threats. Any
member caught breaking the rules would be immediately
removed, without warning or a second chance. Break the
rules and you were out—permanently.

Every one of Protégé's members had something to lose
by coming here. My job was to keep the place invisible.
Where most places thrived on exposure and exclusivity,

mine relied on staying out of the public eye. Whether you were 'happily' married, trying new experiences with a partner, or just into experimental sex, Protégé could accommodate you.

A membership did not guarantee you entry whenever the mood hit. Bookings were still required for all non-VIP members. As of the month before, our membership was up around two thousand, five percent of whom were VIP. Some members came once a year, some once a month. Everybody was different, and there were no attendance obligations. We had people who had been members for months and had yet to experience what the club could offer them.

The club offered regular theme nights, and tonight was the perfect example: public humiliation.

It sounded much more hardcore than it actually was—or maybe I was just desensitized to it. In approximately fifteen minutes, a pretty young thing was going to be suspended in midair wearing nothing but the ropes that would bind her ankles.

It actually surprised me how popular the public

humiliation nights were. Usually theme nights would take place once every few months; this one had turned into somewhat of a monthly thing, though. The waiting list to participate exceeded six months. We had all types of people wanting to watch and wanting to be humiliated. It was all voluntary, and participants could stop at any moment— though they rarely did. I'll admit it: standing anonymously with a crowd of bystanders watching a woman bound and gagged get fucked senseless from every angle was incredibly arousing.

Had I participated? No. Would I? Probably not.

For me, the turn-on was purely a visual thing. Some would say it was disgusting. That it was degrading to both the men and women who were being humiliated. But the thing you needed to remember was, the whole thing was voluntary.

We had so many systems in place to ensure the safety of everyone. It wasn't for everyone, but for those into rough sex and voyeurism, it didn't get any better than this.

One of the most common misconceptions was that we provided sex. This was not a brothel; we did not supply women—or men—for sex. We had several hostesses working at any given time who were strictly non-contact.

We simply provided a place for people to meet other like-minded individuals who were after a little bit of fun. Did I participate? Sometimes, as did other staff members, but we were not paid for our involvement.

Generally, there were three types of members: those who liked to participate, those who liked to watch, and those who liked to be watched.

Which did I fit into? All of the above.

I was very complex when it came to my sexual needs. I knew what I liked, and I was confident in getting that. I thought about Beth, and how she would react to this place. When I first met her, I would have thought she'd like it, but her behavior lately had me doubting that assessment. I laughed at how ridiculous I was being; her reaction to Protégé was the last thing I should have been worrying about.

A rap on the door brought me back to the present.

"Come in."

Alli came in, coffee in hand. She smiled at me, then darted her eyes downward as though she were intimidated by me. I smiled, my eyes following her as she walked over and set the cup down in front of me.

"Thanks, Alli. How are you today?"

"Great thank you, Mr. Hale. You are looking very sexy tonight," she added. Her face colored, and I chuckled. "Oh, I didn't mean—"

"It's okay, Alli. Tell Scarlett I'll be out shortly."

She nodded, and ducked her head before retreating out the door, closing it softly behind her. I took the coffee and sank into my chair, spinning around to face the monitors again. My eyes fell on the judge, who was furiously fisting his erection as he watched the couple fuck through the floor-to-ceiling window.

All "private" rooms at Protégé had window-paned walls, so it was like fucking in a fish bowl. Which was great if you were into voyeurism—and let's face it, who doesn't get turned on at the sight of another couple exploring each other?

After I finished my coffee, I removed my jacket and rolled up the cuffs of my sleeves, showing off my tanned forearms. I walked out the front and scanned the club for Scarlett, spotting her over near the bar, chatting to a couple. Leaning against the wall behind me, I watched her. She was so engaging. Her smile lit up the room. She had the couple hanging off her every word, and more than once the man's eyes drifted down over her short silk dress.

I chuckled to myself. This was exactly why Scarlett was my right-hand man. As shy as she sometimes acted around me, in this place she came to life. It was like she was born to do her job, and she did it fucking well.

"Roman?"

I turned and saw Dahlia, her blue eyes sparkling as she smiled at me. I smiled back and accepted the hug she was offering me.

"Dahlia, so good to see you. How have you been?" I asked. Dahlia had been frequenting the club since its early days, sometimes with her husband, sometimes alone.

"Really good. Andrew's over there." She pointed to one of the corner sofas, where I could see Andrew in a deep conversation with a pretty brunette.

"He looks like he's having fun."

"Well, we both will be in a few minutes when we take her into one of the rooms." She laughed, reached out, and touched my arm. "You could always stop by," she added coyly, a little smile playing on her lips. "I know how much you like to watch."

"Maybe I will," I muttered, watching as she walked away. She walked up to Andrew and the brunette, who stood up, linking her arm around Dahlia's back. Andrew was obviously in for a hot night. Maybe I would stop by later . . .

"Sorry, I didn't see you come in." Scarlett smiled at me, her cheeks flushed from running.

"It's okay. You looked to be in pretty deep conversation over there." I raised my eyebrow.

"Yes, they're new. I was just explaining the ins and outs of everything to them."

"Good work. Are you under control here?"

"Yes. Why?"

I smirked. "Don't ask questions, Scarlett."

She blushed.

I shook my head and walked toward the room Dahlia and Andrew were in. The blood began to rush through me as I tried to rationalize what I was about to do. Why was I feeling guilty? This was so fucked up. Beth and I weren't anything. I wasn't good enough for her, and she'd find that out eventually. Besides that, I didn't want to give this up. The last thing I wanted was to be in a relationship where I felt guilty for doing what felt right for me.

Dahlia looked up and smiled at me. I was about to sit down on one of the provided couches outside the room when she motioned for me to come in. I hesitated, but only for a second. That was all it took me to realize I was doing this.

I sat down in the corner of the room, my leg folded over my knee, just watching. Really, how different was this from watching a video? It was like a play of porn—or a musical, if they started to dance. I chuckled at the thought.

"Something funny?" Dahlia asked. She sauntered over to me, slowly unbuttoning her tight shirt. She slipped it over her shoulders, the fabric slowly sliding down her dark skin. "You sure you don't want to participate?" she teased, already knowing the answer. I never joined in; I was content with just watching.

"I'm fine here, thank you."

"Suit yourself."

She walked back over to the bed that sat in the middle of the room. Dressed in the finest Egyptian cotton sheets, the huge bed could accommodate an orgy of people. And sometimes it did.

Andrew was already naked on the bed, the brunette pressed up against him, naked, her knees apart. She moaned softly as his hands ran over her body, resting on her bare pussy. Lifting her arms, she wrapped them around his neck. She faced my direction, giving me the perfect view of her perky breasts and slender body.

I swallowed as Andrew slid a finger inside her, moving it in and out slowly. Dahlia came around the far side of the bed and began pumping his cock. I shifted in my seat, my pants restricting as arousal began to stir inside me.

Unzipping my fly, I reached inside my boxers and freed my cock. Now fully erect, I fisted the base of my shaft, my hand moving back and forth. Closing my eyes, I imagined Beth kneeling before me, taking my cock in her mouth, her sweet, soft lips working my length while her tongue ran along my shaft.

I gasped, my fist moving faster as I brought my attention back to the show before me. Dahlia lay on her back, her legs spread, while the brunette with the perky little breasts lapped at her pussy. Even from where I was sitting I could see how wet she was.

Andrew began to rub the brunette from behind, his other hand stroking his cock. He rolled on a condom and eased it inside of her ass. She didn't flinch, her mouth not leaving Dahlia for even a second.

Fuck, yeah. There was something so erotic about watching people fuck. I pumped my throbbing cock, precum covering my fingers as I worked from base to tip.

"Fuck," I hissed as I released, my load shooting onto the floor in front of me. Holy shit, that felt good. Standing

up, I fixed my pants and walked out, thinking to myself that
we didn't pay our cleaning staff nearly enough.

***

I had only one thing on my mind when I entered the
house after returning from the club, and that was to call
Beth. I'd been thinking about her all night. Imagining her . .
. Imagining us. I glanced at my phone. After four in the
morning was probably pushing it, but then again, knowing
her, she'd be up. Or out. Possibly getting drunk. Possibly
picking up some random guy to take home and fuck.

A surge of anger rushed through me. A text. I would
send her a text.

Are you awake?

I waited impatiently for her to reply. Five minutes . . .
ten minutes . . . After half an hour, I gave up. If she didn't
want to talk to me, then I wasn't going to wait up half the
night like a pussy. I didn't care how irrational I sounded, or
that it was the middle of the night and there was a very
good chance she was asleep; I wanted to talk to her, and
she wasn't answering. That pissed me off. And I was angry
that it got to me so much.

Storming into the kitchen, I opened the fridge and grabbed a beer. I flicked off the lid and walked into the living room, slumping down on the sofa. The TV was on, but there was nothing worth watching. *Fuck this.* I stood up and went to bed, tipping the untouched beer down the drain in the kitchen on the way.

Chapter Fourteen

Beth

I woke early the next morning, the left side of my bed empty. The soft creases in the sheets were my only proof that it hadn't been a dream. I sighed and closed my eyes, imagining his hands moving all over my body.

I really liked him. A lot. But the problem was, every time we had been intimate, it had been after I'd been drinking quite heavily. The thought of being touched by him—or anyone—while I was sober terrified me. I freaking jumped when his fingers unintentionally brushed past my arm. How could this possibly work without me, at the very least, explaining to him what had happened?

This was not good. I thought having him around might give me something else to focus on, but I was becoming more and more reliant on his company. I could feel my independence slipping away.

I rolled over and reached for my phone. Three text messages and a missed call—all from Roman. I clicked on the first message.

Are you awake?

I checked the time. He'd sent that just after four in the morning. I wondered if he'd left by then. I clicked on the second message.

I'm sorry about yesterday. If I hurt you, I didn't mean it.

That one had been sent at six this morning. Finally I clicked on the last message, not sure what to expect.

Give me a call when you can. I hope you're okay.

I smiled and lay back in the bed.

***

Around midday I got up and showered. I had a meeting at the recording studio to run over a few ideas for my latest album. That in itself didn't bother me, but Ivan would be there. I'd spent weeks combing over my contract, looking for a clause to get out, but he was right—if I fired him, he would sue me, and I could lose everything. I didn't care about my possessions and money; it was the thought of everything going to *him* that made me angry. No matter which way I looked at this, he won.

I clutched my jacket tightly around my waist as I walked inside. Ivan and Sam, my producer, sat in the corner in a heated discussion over something. Just when I thought I'd made it past them unnoticed, Ivan looked up and caught my eye.

"Well, look who finally decided to show up," he said mockingly. "I have no idea where all this attitude is coming from, but if you want to actually continue making a name for yourself in this business, you'd better pull yourself together."

I wanted to slap him. First of all, I *was not* late. Secondly, he had no idea where this was coming from?

Bull-fucking-shit. You *raped* me, you piece-of-shit asshole. You forced yourself on me, and ruined my life.

Every fucking day I relive what you did to me, over and over.

Shaking, I stalked into the dressing room. I shrugged off my jacket and my bag. Bending over the table with my palms flat on the surface, I closed my eyes and breathed.

In, out. In, out.

I refused to break down. Crying in front of him only showed him how much his words affected me. I would not give him any more pleasure than he'd already taken. And that was exactly what I did every time I took his bait.

I stood up and pulled my hair back into a ponytail, tying a black rubber band around it. *You can do this. Show him nothing.*

"So, what are we starting with?" I asked, walking back into the room. I directed my question at Sam.

Ivan studied me, searching for any crack in my mask. His eyes penetrated me, almost daring me to react. On the outside I was cool, calm and collected—the complete opposite of the mess I was feeling internally. Being so close to him . . . I wanted to hide. All I could think of was him, all over me and inside me. Oh God, that smell.

I walked toward the sound booth, anticipating Sam's response. Or at least that's how I hoped it looked. I just needed to get away from Ivan. He was too damn close.

"Okay, run from the top. We just want to play around with the layout of the tracks."

One by one, I ran through the tracks on the album. Three of the songs were set for single release.

I'd written all of them. But that was before. The last two months, I hadn't written anything. It was like my creativity had just dried up.

"Can you go a bit higher with that last note?" asked Sam.

I ran for the melody again, trying to stretch my voice higher, but it cracked.

"Give it another go," he suggested.

I nodded, and then had a thought. "I think we should change the order of those last few lines. I can't get that note, and I'm not going on stage and making a fool of myself." I sighed, rubbing my forehead to ease the headache I felt coming on.

"That won't work," replied Sam, very matter of fact.

"Who wrote the damn song? If I think a few lines should be altered, then decision made." I hadn't meant to sound so crabby. I was in a foul mood and just wanted the session to be over.

I saw Ivan lean over and whisper something in Sam's ear. What was he saying? Probably putting me down or trying to wreck my credibility—not that I needed him to do that. I managed it quite well on my own.

"Okay, maybe we'll leave it for now. I can fix the inconsistencies later. But you might want to lay off some of the late nights, considering the live shows you have coming up." He said it nicely, but it still hurt.

I glared at Ivan, positive that he had put the excuse of my lifestyle into Sam's head.

And besides, my live shows were freaking weeks away. My face burned as I nodded stiffly. I didn't like being chastised. And that's how it felt. More than that, I didn't want Ivan interfering in my life any more than he already had.

"Are we done here?"

"Sure."

I saw the look they exchanged, and stalked off to the changing room.

***

I walked out from the dressing room, relieved that both of them had gone. Seeing Ivan every fucking day was too much; I couldn't cope anymore. The way he looked at me with that smug little smile made me furious. I so badly wanted to walk over to him and punch him in the balls, just to wipe that expression off his disgusting little face. Everything about him made me sick.

Shit. My jacket. I raced back into the dressing room to retrieve it. Pulling it on, my mind was still in overdrive. A noise directly behind me scared the hell out of me. I spun around and came face-to-face with Ivan.

"What the fuck was that scene out there, Bethy?" he

snarled, obviously angry about my little outburst.

"I don't know what you mean. I was just suggesting—
"

"Well, don't." He took a step toward me, his eyes traveling over my breasts.

I shivered, both scared and nervous at his close proximity to me. I leveled my eyes at him, my expression cool. *I refuse to let him see how terrified I am of him.*

"Can you at least try to be professional when you're at work, honey?"

I turned around, my eyes wide as Ivan confronted me in the changing room. Immediately, my eyes darted around the room, looking for an escape. My hands curled into balls as they hung beside me, ready to react if I needed them to.

"What do you want? You shouldn't be in here." What if I'd been changing? I shuddered at the thought of him seeing any more of my body than he already had.

"That's the thing, darling: I can go anywhere I want. I thought you would've learned that by now." His eyes laughed at me as I stood there struggling to stay in control.

I glared at him, my expression stony. Inside was a crying mess. "Just leave it, Ivan. Just leave me alone," I muttered, swallowing hard. *Is Sam still here?* I'd thought Ivan had gone, and he hadn't. What were the chances? Would he hear me if I screamed?

"I won't fucking leave you alone. You do as I say, you hear me? If I ask you to get down on your knees and fucking beg, then that's what you do. Understand?"

I blinked back tears. I wasn't sure how much longer I could hold off the flood of emotion that was waiting to pour out of me, but I damn sure wasn't going to cry in front of him.

"Whatever," I muttered. "I just thought—"

"Well, don't. You're not here to think—thank fucking Christ for that. We'd all be in the shit if we were dependent on your little mind." He laughed, as if his joke was actually funny.

I scowled at him, my body shaking as I fought hard not to react. Because that's what he wanted: he wanted to see that he was getting to me.

His demeanor changed, and he smiled. "Bethy, you need to relax. Maybe you need to have a little more fun? I'd be happy to help you out with that. It worked so well the last time, you know," he said, his hand reaching for a loose strand of hair that had fallen across my face.

I ducked back, my heart racing. I wanted to scream.

He wasn't going to touch me *ever* again.

Picking up my bag, I pushed past him, hurling him into the bench near the lockers. I raced for the door, not checking behind me to see if he was following. I just needed to get out of there.

Walk. Just keep walking. Walk until he can't get to you anymore. Do not let him get to you.

It was easier said than done; Ivan got to me on a daily basis. As I pushed my way through the door and outside, his voice echoed through the studio.

"Don't forget, honey, I know where you live. Maybe I'll drop by and say hello."

That sick fuck. Was that an empty threat, or was he really planning on coming after me again? I didn't want to find out.

***

By the time I arrived home, the panic had subsided, but I wasn't ready to be alone. I weighed up my options: I could either call Roman, or I could call Roman. I turned my bag inside out looking for my phone, finally locating it at the very bottom. I scrolled through my contacts until his name showed up. Hitting call, I waited for him to answer. Or not answer. Panic rose inside me. What if he didn't answer? I couldn't stay there alone, not right then. If I did, I'd lose my mind.

"Hello?"

"Roman," I blurted out. I hadn't been ready for him to answer, and now I had no idea what the hell to say.

"Beth." He sounded genuinely pleased to hear from me.

I relaxed, actually managing to breathe.

"How are you? Is everything okay?"

"Everything's fine," I said, a little too quickly. "I was just wondering if maybe you wanted to meet for coffee?"

"A coffee?" he repeated.

"Yes. Coffee. It's what people have sometimes over a discussion to get to know each other better."

"You want to get to know me?"

"Roman, either you want to or you don't."

"Okay, I'm sorry. I'd love to meet you for coffee. Or better yet, how about I treat you to a hot chocolate that is so good it will make you orgasm?"

I laughed. "How can I say no to that?"

Chapter Fifteen

Beth

"Glad you could make it."

I turned around and smiled. Roman approached me, a sexy smile working across his lips as he looked me over. I lowered my eyes, loving the way I felt when I was around him.

"How could I pass up the promise of a hot chocolate that will make me orgasm?" I teased. I felt myself relax. See, I could do this. It was just talking. Just two friends meeting for a drink.

"Hey, I make no guarantees, but should this fail, I am prepared to honor the promise myself." He chuckled as my face went red. Was that a joke? I didn't want to ask, afraid of what the response would be.

"I'm not embarrassing you, am I?" He smirked.

"No," I said smugly. "I'm just embarrassed on your behalf at that poor pickup line."

He laughed loudly. "Well thank you, but I don't need your pity. Besides, I thought that line was pretty smooth," he returned, as the waitress walked over to our table.

***

I dug my spoon down to the bottom of the mug, scooping up a mountain of creamy goodness. Okay, I had to admit: this was damn good. I could quite easily become addicted. I looked up at Roman, who was staring at me. His mouth twitched, like he wanted to say something.

"What?"

"Nothing. You just have a little . . ." He reached over to my chin, catching a rogue drop of cream. His eyes gleamed as he lifted his thumb to my mouth. "You may as well finish it." I giggled and parted my mouth. He slipped his thumb inside, his insanely dark eyes narrowing in on me as I sucked it gently.

Placing his arm back down in his lap, he shook his head and laughed. "You better watch yourself, Ms. Masters. You don't want to wind me up."

"I don't?" I teased. I liked this. I was relaxed and playful. Slowly, I was coming out of my shell. Now if only I could be consistent. I was running more hot-and-cold these days than Katy freaking Perry.

It hit me that I still knew very little about him.

"So, who are you, Roman?"

"Who am I?" He leaned back in the booth and cocked his head to the side. "I'm just a guy, Beth. There's nothing special about me. I don't know what to tell you." He let out a laugh. *Was it just me, or did that question make him go all weird?*

"I'd say there is plenty special about you. But I want to know who you are. What makes you tick. Are you close with your family? I feel like everything has been about me. I want to hear about you."

"Okay." He nodded. "You present an impressive argument. My parents are dead. I have a brother I never see, and I'm not much for friendships." He held my gaze. I felt like I was being dragged into his soul. "But for pretty little pop stars, I like to make an exception," he added softly.

He thought I was pretty? I wondered if he could hear the pounding in my chest. *God, I hope I'm not smiling like an idiot right now.*

"So we're friends now?"

"We're something," he finally replied. Something. I liked something more than I liked friendship. Something suggested hope, and I needed that right now.

"I'm sorry about your parents," I offered.

He shrugged. "It's okay. I've dealt with it and moved on." The tone of his voice had changed, and I got the feeling that the subject of his family was closed for discussion. As curious as I was, I didn't want to press him.

"Still, I don't know much about you. You come across as very mysterious." I narrowed my eyes and pointed my spoon at him accusingly.

He laughed and nodded. "I guess you're right. So ask me something else then. Anything." He stirred his coffee while he waited patiently for me to speak.

"Your strongest memory from age ten."

"What?" he laughed, amused by the randomness of my question.

"Go," I ordered, waving my hand at him.

"Give me a minute," he chuckled, shaking his head. "Okay. Breaking the neighbors' window with my spud gun. And possibly breaking a ten-thousand-dollar vase in the process."

"What?" I giggled, covering my mouth. "What the hell is a spud gun?"

His eyes widened. He pointed to my cup. "Drink up," he ordered.

"What, why?"

"Don't argue, just hurry up."

I did as he said. It was hard work downing a cup of chocolate and cream without getting it all over my face. He shook his head and handed me his napkin. I took it and wiped my mouth, disappointed he didn't offer me his thumb again.

"Let's go." He stood up and threw a twenty on the table. Grabbing my hand, he all but dragged me out of the restaurant.

"Where are we going?" I laughed, getting into the car.

"Well, first stop is the hardware store, and then the grocer's."

What the hell?

The hardware store was a few blocks down from the restaurant. We pulled into the parking lot. Roman pointed across the road. "You go over there and buy a sack of potatoes and a can of deodorant."

"Are you saying I smell?" I joked.

He rolled his eyes and shook his head. "You smell beautiful. Now go."

All right. I walked across the road while he went into the hardware store. Picking out a few nice potatoes, I bagged them and then went hunting for some deodorant, grabbing the first can I saw.

I met Roman back at the car. Holding up my purchases, I grinned.

"Good work. Okay, now let's go." We got in the car and took off. I still had no idea where we were going, though I was smart enough to have figured out what we'd be doing.

***

We pulled up at a clearing beside Mason's Point, just around the corner from my house. I waited while Roman gathered our things, laying them out on the hood of the car.

The lake was so peaceful—not so much as a ripple across the smooth surface. It almost looked like a layer of glass. Tall, jagged rocks surrounded the clearing, making it not the safest spot to swim. Not that that stopped the thrill-seekers who liked to climb to the top of the point and dive into the water.

"Beth." I turned to see Roman gesturing to me. "This is a potato cannon." He sounded so proud as he held up what looked like a few bits of pipe glued together.

"Wow, looks great," I offered brightly.

He narrowed his eyes at me. "Don't patronize me, Ms. Masters," he warned, reaching for a potato. "It's not impressive yet, but watch this." He loaded the potato down the end of the pipe and aimed it out over the lake.

I jumped as it fired, sending a flaming potato flying through the air. Holy shit! That had to have gone two hundred yards.

"Oh, I'm so giving that a try," I said, practically jumping up and down.

He laughed and handed it to me. I aimed the pipe into the air and pressed the release, just like he'd done. I squealed as the potato fired out of the pipe in a ball of flames, dropping the cannon onto the sand. Roman doubled over with laughter, only stopping when I scowled at him.

Still chuckling, he leaned down to retrieve it. "So, you now know a hundred percent more about me than you did an hour ago," he announced with a cheeky grin.

"Right, but a hundred percent of nothing still isn't that much," I pointed out.

"True." He thought for a moment. "Okay, how about this? See that island out there?" He pointed to a narrow sand bunker about two hundred and fifty yards from the shore. "We each have a shot. If you get it over the island, then you can ask me a question. But if you don't you need to answer one."

"And if I don't want to answer the question?" I asked nervously. I could just imagine what he'd ask me: things I didn't want to answer—things I wasn't ready to answer.

He smiled mischievously. "That's where the fun begins. If you don't want to answer, no problems. You just have to complete a dare."

"A dare?" I repeated, laughing. I couldn't remember the last time I'd played a game of Truth or Dare. Okay. "You're on." He handed the spud gun back to me. Trying not to show my nerves, I aimed it carefully and fired. I watched as a potato bounded through the air. "Come on, come on. Yes!" I threw my arms up and started cheering, dancing circles around him.

He shook his head and laughed. "Nice shot."

"I bet you thought you were pretty safe, huh?" I grinned.

"No. I was pretty sure you could handle your way around a piece of pipe this long."

I glowered at him and he laughed harder.

"So, ask your question," he managed to say.

"Okay," I began. "How do you know Scarlett? And why did you want to watch us?" I asked him, blushing.

He grinned, pulling his eyebrows together. Maybe he hadn't been expecting that. "What man wouldn't want to watch two women? Scarlett is an old friend."

"An old friend?" I said suspiciously. "She looks younger than me."

He laughed, but didn't respond.

"What else do you want with me? I mean, why are you

here?"

"Honestly, Beth? There are so many things I want to do with you and *to* you and watch have done to you, but I'm hesitant about scaring you off."

Watch done to me? What did that mean? The mere thought stirred an aching between my legs.

"Do I seem like the kind of girl who is easily scared away?"

"No, but you do seem lost. I don't know what's gone on in your past, but I feel like you're running from something."

Oh, God. *Here we go again*. He wanted to save me. Fuck, I knew how to pick them.

Sighing, I gathered my things and stood up. He gaped in surprise.

"I told you, Roman: I don't need a babysitter. When you can accept that, then give me a call."

Chapter Sixteen

Roman

Groaning, I buried my head under the pile of cushions taking up the end of the sofa I was lying on. Fuck. *If you mess with her, he is going to kill you.* All I'd had to do was keep an eye on her and report back that she was okay. That was it. And in return, I'd have enough to pay off the debt for the club. It was fucking easy money, and I was screwing it all up because my heart was being a fuckwit.

"Fuck!" I yelled. I picked up the lamp on my desk and threw it at the wall, and then brought my fists down on the desk so hard I broke through the top layer of glass.

Shit. I watched as blood trickled from the gash on the edge of my palm, tiny little droplets falling onto the cream-colored rug under me.

"Are you okay?" Scarlett came bursting through the door. She glanced from the shattered lamp to my hand.

"Yep. Fine," I said curtly. Her face dropped, and I sighed. Right now I couldn't handle another emotional woman. "I'm sorry. This job is getting to me, that's all."

"Here," she said, walking over to me. Taking my hand in hers, she sighed. "Let me clean this up for you. Come down to the kitchen."

I nodded, ripping my shirt off and tying it around my hand like a makeshift bandage.

"What are you doing? Throwing lamps at the wall?" she asked as she sat me down at the table and went to retrieve a bandage.

I scowled at Scarlett. "And this is your business because . . .?"

"Because believe it or not, I consider you a friend. I don't want to see you like this. Messed up over some girl."

"Leave her out of this."

"Because you are? Listen, Roman, have you even

thought about how she is going to react when she finds out you have been deceiving her? Because that's what this is, and that's exactly how she's going to see it."

"No offense, Scarlett, but when I want your advice, I'll ask for it," I snapped.

"What's that supposed to mean?" she asked, her hands dropping to her hips. She pouted, her mouth falling into a frown. She was hurt and I didn't blame her; I was being an asshole.

"I'm sorry. I'm just stressed." I glanced down at my bandaged hand. "Thanks for this." I gave her a smile, then left her in the kitchen.

***

"I'm sorry."

It had taken me all afternoon to call her, to work up the courage to say those two little words. I sat in my office, waiting for her to say something. Anything. All I knew was that whatever this was, I didn't want to ruin it.

"It's okay," she said softly. "Look, I get it. I do. But I

need you to stop trying to fix me, okay?"

"Okay." I wasn't convinced I could keep that promise, but I was willing to try. "Come meet me? I'll send a cab. Let me cook for you."

"You cook?" I could hear the laughter in her voice.

"Well, no. Not well, anyway. Okay, it might be safer if I order us some takeout, but don't let that keep you away."

"Okay. I'll come over."

***

She was right on time. Dead-on six o'clock, the doorbell rang.

I'd convinced Scarlett to go out for the night. I knew she wouldn't be home until early morning, because she was scheduled at the club.

I checked my reflection in the mirror on my way to answering the door. I scrubbed up pretty well. I wore loose-fitting jeans, which I paired with a long-sleeved black shirt. I was in pretty good shape, considering my age. Not that thirty-two was old, but I certainly felt older than I imagined most people my age felt. I opened the door.

"Hi." Beth smiled at me. Holy shit. She was fucking gorgeous. This was as casually dressed as I'd seen her, yet she took my breath away. Her tight jeans hugged her curves, displaying her beautiful figure. She wore an emerald-green wrap-around top, and her blonde hair, slightly curled, hung in waves around her face.

"Hey. Come in," I said, realizing I was just standing there like an idiot.

She smiled and squeezed past me, her sweet musky perfume engulfing me.

"You're fucking gorgeous," I muttered, sweeping her into my arms. I kissed her passionately, my lips pressing against hers.

Smiling, she pulled away and surveyed me. "You don't look too bad yourself."

Reaching out for her hand, I pulled her towards me, wrapping her arms around my waist. I tilted my head and kissed her again. Her lips glided over mine. I kept hold of her hand and led her inside.

"Wow, your house is beautiful," she murmured, her head tilted towards the ceiling.

"Thanks. It's been in the family for years. I spent a fortune fixing it up after my parents died."

She hesitated, her eyes clouding over.

"What is it?"

"Why?" she asked. "I mean, you told me you didn't have the best childhood. Why would you keep the house, and spend so much money restoring it?"

"Just because my childhood wasn't perfect doesn't mean I didn't love them." It was hard to explain. Sometimes it feels like bad love is better than no love, and the same can be said for family: no matter how often I felt unwanted, no matter how many times my best wasn't good enough, having a family was still better than not having a family.

"I wish I shared your sentiment." Her eyes lowered. Placing my hand around her shoulders, I lifted her chin up until her eyes met mine.

"Your situation was worse than mine. What you went through with your mother and then your sister, and then having to support yourself... I don't blame you for thinking you'd be better off alone."

"I just find it hard to trust people. I've been taken advantage of so many times..."

"As hard as it is, you need to let people in."

"I'm trying," she whispered. "So what's for dinner? Did you cook?"

I chuckled. "Trust me, you don't want to taste my cooking. Scarlett prepared this."

"Scarlett?" Beth said, taken aback.

Right: we hadn't got to the conversation just yet about Scarlett living with me. I moved around the counter until I stood behind Beth. Sweeping her hair over to one side, I began to kiss her neck. "Yes. Scarlett is my assistant. She lives with me."

"She lives with you?" She spun the barstool until she was facing me.

"Didn't I mention that?" I said casually. I could tell by the way she was narrowing her eyes at me that I wasn't going to get out of this one that easily. "Look, Scarlett is just a friend. Not even a friend, more of an associate. She works for me, that's it."

"Have you slept with her?"

I chuckled. "Beth, you've done more with her than I have."

She blushed. My cock began to throb as I remembered that night: Beth, spread out on the sofa, crying out as Scarlett fingered her.

"You're thinking about that night, aren't you?" she accused, rubbing over my erection.

For as long as you keep doing that, I will be. Leaning down, I kissed her roughly, my mouth massaging hers. Pushing her head to one side, I ran my tongue along the curve of her neck, kissing the soft skin up to her ear lobe. I took it in my mouth and began to suck. She let out a cry before turning so our lips met.

"Dinner is going to get cold," I mumbled, my tongue

wrestling against hers.

"Then I guess we better eat."

The only thing I wanted to eat was her. Pushing apart her legs, I thrust my fingers inside her panties. She stiffened, pressing her legs together as she forced my hand out. "I'm, uh, kind of really hungry."

Wow. Shot down. Maybe I was losing my touch.

"Then I guess we'd better eat," I replied with a little too much enthusiasm. Just like that, the mood completely changed; things between us felt awkward and strange.

"Can I help?" she asked, eyeing me.

"There is a bottle of wine in the fridge you can open," I said. I took the tray of lasagna from the oven and sat it on the stove.

"Shit!"

I looked over at Beth. Blood dripped from her hand onto the white tiles. Grabbing a handful of paper towels, I pressed them onto the palm of her hand and closed her fingers into a fist around it.

"What have you done?" I said, stroking her cheek.

She shook her head. "I was trying to get the damn top off the wine."

I looked over at the bottle of unopened wine. The top looked as though it'd been hacked with a box cutter. I swallowed a laugh. She was in a foul mood as it was, and me finding this funny wasn't going to help things.

I lifted the paper towel carefully to survey the damage. The tiny cut had seemed worse than it actually was, considering the amount of blood that had come out of it. I grabbed a handful of fresh paper towels and ran it under the water. I gently washed away the blood.

"I don't think I have any Band-Aids," I said apologetically.

She smiled. "In my bag, there is a pocket inside. You'll find some in there."

I was impressed. "You're prepared."

"No," she laughed. "Just clumsy. And wearing heels, trust me, Band-Aids are a necessity."

I walked over to her bag and found the Band-Aids in the pocket, just as she'd described.

Something caught my eye. Though I couldn't see much of it, I could clearly make out the title of the pamphlet shoved inside of her bag.

Sexual Assault.

Oh, God, no. Fuck. My heart raced as random moments popped into my head. The signs, they'd all been there. The changes in her behavior, her issues with intimacy. Even her drinking and all night partying should've alerted me that something was seriously wrong.

How could I have missed this?

"No luck?"

Shit—the Band-Aids. I closed her bag and walked back over, holding up what looked to be *Dora the Explorer* Band-Aids.

"They were the only ones I could find," she said defensively.

"Sure," I teased. What was I supposed to do now? Did

I mention what I'd seen? Did I wait for her to bring it up? If I was waiting for her, I could be waiting forever. But the last thing I wanted to do was push her away.

I carefully positioned the Band-Aid over the cut.

"There. All fixed."

"Thanks." She grinned, throwing the paper towels into the trash. "Dinner smells nice."

"Why don't you sit down while I finish this?" I took the wine and opened it, pouring it into two glasses. Sliding hers across the kitchen counter, I caught her eye. A surge of anger rushed through me. What had happened to her? Had it been recent? I wanted to hold her in my arms and tell her everything would be fine, but she'd made it clear she didn't need fixing. I had no idea what to do here.

Serving up the lasagna, I carried both dishes over to the table. Beth joined me with our drinks. She sat down and began eating. My appetite had disappeared the moment I saw that pamphlet.

"Not hungry?" Beth asked, covering her mouth.

"Not really," I muttered. I couldn't do this. I needed to know. She was going to be pissed eventually when she realized I knew. "Beth, I saw the brochure on sexual assault in your bag." *Good one, Roman. Just blurt it out.*

She froze, her expression one I could only describe as terror. Immediately, I regretted bringing it up. I should have waited until she told me. It was her choice whether or not she wanted me to know, and I'd just taken that from her.

"I'm sorry—"

"Don't," she cut in. "Don't do that. Don't feel sorry for me. I can't handle your pity." She dropped her fork and stood up, the legs of the chair dragging over the tiled floor. "I have to go."

"Beth, wait!" I took off after her, cutting her off at the front door. Pulling her into my arms, I held her as she fought me. "Let me help you. Please just don't push me away." Slowly, her movements became less and less until she leaned against me, defeated.

She was crying. I walked her over to the sofa and sat her down next to me, cradling her in my arms. I didn't press her to talk to me; I'd already pushed her too hard, too soon.

"You don't have to talk to me, but don't shut me out,"
I murmured.

She didn't say anything as she sat slumped over,
staring off into nothing. Stroking her hair, I kissed her
forehead. As strong as my desire was to help her, so help
me God, if I found out who hurt her, his life would not be
worth living. I'd make sure he paid for this.

"I was raped."

My heart skipped. Turning to her, I waited for her to
continue. It had taken her over an hour to utter those three
little words.

She reached for my hand and held it tightly. "It
happened a while ago. About a year. I didn't know him,
and I didn't see his face. I thought I was over it…or at least
dealing with it. But apparently I'm not."

"Did you report it?" I asked, my voice hoarse.

She shook her head. "No. You're the first person I've
told."

"Beth…" I stopped, unsure of what to say. *I'm sorry you were raped?* Nothing sounded like enough. There weren't words to describe how I was feeling. I didn't want to pity her, but I did. And the idea that some gutless asshole had gotten away with this made my blood boil.

I wanted to hunt him down and skin him alive.

"I'm sorry, Roman. There's not much else to say. I don't remember much of it. It happened, and I can't change that." She shrugged. This girl amazed me. What strength she had, dealing with an assault on her own, with little to no support. She hesitated, then turned to me. "Roman, I'm going to go. I think I just want to go home and sleep."

I shook my head.

"You're not going anywhere tonight. Sleep here. I'll stay on the sofa. You can have my bed."

"No—"

"This isn't negotiable, Beth. Come with me."

She took my hand.

I led her down the hall to my room. "If you want

anything, please let me know."

She smiled and wrapped her arms around me. Her head rested on my chest as my hands stroked her head.

I kissed her softly. "Sleep well."

Chapter Seventeen

Beth

My eyes fluttered open, the bright sunlight streaming through the partially closed curtains nearly blinding me. I sat up, realizing this wasn't my room. I glanced down, relieved to find that I was dressed in my tank and panties.

Roman. Lying back down, everything from the previous night came back to me, from me freaking out, to explaining to him that I'd been raped. I cursed myself. Why had I told him? Now he had even more reason to treat me like a victim. At least he didn't know how recent it had been. He had assumed it had happened a year ago, and I let him believe that.

Grabbing hold of the bedspread, I pulled it over my face and groaned.

"What the hell are you doing?"

I peeked out from my blanket fort. Roman stood beside the bed, a mug in his hand and a bemused expression on his face.

"Um, just regretting last night," I said truthfully.

"What's to regret?" he asked, sitting down beside me. He placed the mug on the bedside table. "Oh. You regret telling me."

"No, it's not that," I said. What was the point in lying? "Well, okay. Yes. Look, I like you. I like that you make me feel like normal Beth. I'm worried that this will give you even more reason . . ." I stopped, not wanting to come across as ungrateful. I liked that he wanted to look after me, I really did, but at the same time, I needed to get my independence back.

"And you think I'll treat you differently now?" he guessed.

"Won't you?"

He didn't answer. Reaching for my hand, his fingers

entwined with mine. He leaned down, his lips melting into me. All my fears dissipated with that one kiss—a long, sensual, passionate kiss.

"Beth, when you're ready to move this forward, I'm ready. In the meantime, I'm going to take my time getting to know every single part of you."

I whimpered softly, closing my eyes as his fingers trailed over my tank, stopping at my panties. God, that felt so good. I went from hot to cold in a matter of seconds, and I hated it. The way he'd touched me just now had made me feel incredibly sexy, yet last night I'd totally freaked out.

"Have your coffee. I have to go out for a while, but you're welcome to stay here as long as you like." He stood up, staring hard at me once more.

"Roman?" I said as he walked out.

He turned.

"Thank you."

***

I woke up a few hours later, surprised that I had fallen

back asleep. I felt the bed beside me for my phone. A text from Ivan. No, wait—two texts from Ivan. *Great.*

I grimaced as I clicked "open," my heart racing. What the hell did he want now? It wasn't enough that I had to put up with him at work, but now he was bothering me on my days off?

You have a reading in LA next week for the movie. Have you read the script? I suggest you learn the first few scenes. We don't want you fucking this up.

"I haven't even agreed to audition yet," I muttered, clicking on the second text.

And I'll need you to do me a favor while you're there.

What was I, his fucking assistant? He could run his own damn errands. I was about to flick the phone back on the bed when I saw I had an unread email. I clicked on it.

Beth,

I just wanted you to know I'm thinking of you. I'm giving you the space you need, but please remember I'm

here if you need me. I miss my friend.

Love,

Coop

I miss my friend. Boy, did I miss him too. But we couldn't just go back to how things were. Too much had happened.

I stared at the email. I so badly wanted to call him. With everything that was going on, and now Roman . . . I needed someone to talk to. I needed my friend back. I clicked reply.

The blank screen stared back at me. What was I supposed to write? *Hey, okay let's give it a go?* After all the pushing away I had done, now I turn around and want him back?

I miss you too. I want things to be the way they were, more than anything. Can we start slow?

I hit send before I could change my mind. Had I really just done that? I wondered what now. If he called, or wanted to meet, could I handle that? Probably not.

Eventually, but not yet.

I climbed out of the bed and dressed in yesterday's clothes. Making my way downstairs, I found the kitchen and made myself a fresh coffee. My email was on loud alert, but that didn't stop me from refreshing it every ten seconds.

I turned on the TV and sank down on the sofa, stretching myself out as I ran over the possible responses from Coop. *Hurry up and reply already.* My phone began to vibrate. Gingerly, I picked it up. Sure enough, there was a text from Coop.

You have no idea how happy you've just made me. As slow as you want, Beth.

I couldn't help but smile.

Texting is good. I can handle that.

A surge of relief flooded through me. It wasn't much, but it was a start. Fixing things with Coop gave me hope that I might actually be able to move on from that night.

So . . . how are you doing?

I laughed. How was I doing? Things were pretty shitty. But they were better than they had been a couple of weeks ago.

I'm okay. I'm sorry. About everything. I shouldn't have pushed you away like I did.

He replied right away.

I'm just glad you're talking to me now. Or at least typing to me.

I laughed, setting my phone down. For two months I had pushed him away. He made one mistake; but the only person to blame for what happened that night was Ivan. I was beginning to realize that.

***

Just after lunch, Scarlett came home, her hands filled with shopping. She gave me a friendly smile, but I could see she felt as awkward as I did. I felt obliged to sit in the kitchen and attempt conversation as she unpacked. Which was hard, because I couldn't look at her without remembering her naked with her fingers inside me. And that made me want to cringe.

"So, are you and Roman close?" I asked. Hell, I'll admit it: I was curious to hear her view on their relationship. These things didn't always match up.

She snorted. "I've known him for a few years, but I would barely call us friends." She turned to me. "He's a very private man. He's been through some things, and I think he finds it hard to open up sometimes. But he's a good guy. A good guy who has made some wrong decisions in the past and learned from them."

What did she mean by that? *Wrong decisions*—that sounded very ominous. I didn't ask any more, I just sat there thinking about all the wrong decisions I'd made in my life. Who was I to judge?

"I better get going," I said. I stood up and grabbed my bag. "It was nice seeing you again."

"You too, Beth. I'm sure I'll see you again soon."

***

"Did you have fun?" he asked me.

I nodded. I always had fun with him.

Since our 'talk' about the rape, he had been super patient and supportive. I always made the first move, and I felt confident that if things went too far, he would stop. That trust meant the world to me. I trusted him like I did no other. Having someone know about what had happened was a relief. It was no longer just Ivan and I who knew, and in a weird way, that made me feel stronger—like he had less power over me.

***

I invited him inside. After a coffee, I led him into the bedroom.

Slowly, I began to unbutton his shirt. He gazed down at me, lifting his hands to catch my wrists.

"I'm not sleeping with you, Beth. Not yet. Not until you're ready."

"What if I *am* ready?" I pouted.

"Then a little longer isn't going to hurt, is it?"

"It's not like we haven't had sex before," I protested. "And if things get...hard, I trust you to stop."

He shook his head. "Not tonight." He curved his hand around the back of my neck and kissed me. His lips felt amazing against mine. This was doing nothing to ease the need I had for him. "I'd love nothing more than to be inside you right now, Beth, but the next time I do that, it's going to feel right."

I pulled away from him. Why did I feel rejected? Staring at him, I lifted my dress over my head and tossed it on the floor. He breathed in sharply as he took in my body. I reached behind my back and unclipped my bra, letting that, too, fall away.

"You may not want to have sex with me," I began, walking over to the bed, "but you can't stop me from touching myself in front of you."

I had him, and he knew it. I could tell from the look of desire in his eyes and the way his jaw had tensed. Slowly, I peeled off my panties and kicked them aside. Kneeling on the bed with my legs parted, I began to touch my bare pussy.

"You like this?" I asked him, dipping my finger inside myself.

"You're not playing fair, Beth."

I let out a little moan as I rubbed my breasts, squeezing my nipples as I worked my finger in and out of my wet pussy. He moved toward me at a snail's pace, his eyes not leaving mine. The effect my little performance was having on him was obvious by the large bulge in his pants.

I smiled as he lowered himself down to me. *I won. Don't mess with Beth.*

But then he placed a soft kiss on my forehead and smiled at me.

"Goodnight, Beth," he murmured, his eyes laughing at me.

My mouth dropped open. I watched him leave my room, closing the door behind him without so much as a glance back at me. I threw myself back on the bed, so angry. I snorted—angry at what? Finding the only guy in the world who refused to rush into sex with a rape victim?

How could I possibly stay angry at him? The answer was I couldn't.

Chapter Eighteen

Beth

A day without seeing Roman was like a day without oxygen: I struggled to survive. He'd had things to do, apparently, that didn't involve me.

Studying myself in the mirror, I nodded with satisfaction. Let's see him pass on my advances tonight. The intercom buzzed, and I raced to let him in. By the time he reached my door I was ready, my purse in hand and my feet slipping into my heels.

"You look stunning," he mumbled, leaning over to kiss me.

I grinned. With no clue where we were headed, I'd thrown on a silk dress that hung just above the knee and a pair of strappy heels.

"Are you going to tell me where we're going?" I asked as we walked to his car—if you could even call it a car. The sporty, black, metal contraption parked in my driveway was not his usual transportation, and it must have cost a fortune.

"Impressed?" he asked as he opened the door for me.

I shrugged. "You're talking to one of the highest earners in the country last year. Material things don't impress me." I smirked.

He raised his eyebrows as he pushed the door shut. "So, what does impress you then, Beth?"

I thought for a moment. "A man who knows how to treat a woman. Someone who thinks before they act. Someone who thinks of others before they act."

"That shouldn't be something that impresses. That should be standard behavior."

"Unfortunately, not all men see it that way." I shrugged, determined not to put a damper on our night. "So, where did you get the car?"

He laughed. "Mine is being serviced. This belongs to a friend."

"Nice friend," I joked. "So, where is it we're going?" I asked.

Roman smirked at me and shook his head. "Be patient. You'll find out soon enough."

I sank further back into my seat and pouted. I didn't like surprises. The only surprises I'd received growing up were bad ones. Like the time Mom's boyfriend got high and slayed my pet dog in the living room. Walking in on that at age ten wasn't a good surprise.

Or when he'd try to climb into bed with me in the middle of the night. Nothing ever happened, thank God. He'd always passed out from the alcohol as soon as his head hit my pillow, but that didn't stop me from sleeping with a knife under my mattress, just in case.

I glanced over at Roman, who was concentrating on the road. His dark hair was cropped short against his tanned skin. His jaw twitched as he focused, oblivious to my attention. I smiled and turned away, leaning my elbow against the door of the car.

We pulled up outside a small burger shack. I screwed up my nose, glancing down at my twelve-hundred-dollar outfit.

Roman chuckled. "I told you, you look stunning."

"Maybe, but I think I'm a bit overdressed."

"So undress then," he said with a smirk.

I narrowed my eyes at him, but couldn't help but smile. "You wish," I shot back.

"You're right, I do."

I rolled my eyes and got out of the car, following him into the diner. We were seated at a booth near the door. I slid across the wooden seat and reached for a menu. For once, I was actually starving.

"What do you recommend here?" I asked him, poring over the offerings.

Double beef and bacon cheeseburger. The thought made my mouth water.

"It's all pretty good. I think I'll go with a ranch

special. You?"

"The double beef and bacon burger?" I asked, blushing.

"Well, someone has an appetite," he chuckled, raising his eyebrows at me.

I shrugged. "I like my meat," I replied.

He raised his eyebrows and I blushed. I knew exactly where his mind had gone.

Our dinner came out and we chowed it down. It was surprisingly good. I'd even stopped caring about being overdressed; I was just focused on Roman and the great time I was having.

"Dessert?" he asked with a smile.

"God, no," I groaned, clutching my stomach. "I think I ate a whole cow just then."

"I'm actually impressed you got through the whole thing," he laughed.

So was I. And now I was regretting it. My stomach

made a weird gurgling noise. I looked up, horrified. Roman began to laugh hysterically.

"It's not funny," I whined, a smile creeping onto my face.

"Come on. Let's get you home. I think you'll need to hibernate for a month after that meal."

***

"Do you want to come in?" I asked him. We stood by my front gate, and after spending the last ten minutes making out, I wanted to move things forward.

"I have an early start tomorrow," he said, shaking his head.

"It's barely eight," I replied, frowning. I knew what he was doing: he didn't want to pressure me. But what happened when I want things to go further? Like right now?

"I have a very early start tomorrow morning."

"Fine," I huffed. "Well, I'm going in. Maybe I'll see you tomorrow."

He took my hand and placed it on his lips, kissing me softly. My anger melted away as I stared into those brown eyes.

"Don't be angry at me because I want to make sure you're okay."

"I'm not angry. I'm frustrated. There is a difference."

"We don't need to rush this, Beth. I'm not going anywhere." He moved forward, cupping my face in his hands as he kissed me. "I'll call you tomorrow."

I nodded and watched him leave. I stood by the gate until his car disappeared around the bend. Leaning back against the metal bars, I sighed.

How could I stay angry at the only person who'd ever had my best interests at heart?

Chapter Nineteen

Roman

"How old are you here?" I asked, smiling at the photo. The little girl was laughing, her blonde curls out of control around her round face.

She grabbed the picture from me and studied it.

"About three, I think." She smiled and leaned back against me. "The only good memories I have of Mom were when I was three or four. She used to play tea party with me. I had the cutest little plastic tea set. I loved the hell out of that thing."

We sat on the floor in the living room, going through her childhood memories. It saddened me that, good and bad, they all fit in a small shoebox. A few pictures, some childhood drawings, a small stuffed bear...that was it. A whole lifetime, and that was all she had to show for it.

"Let's go out." I got to my feet and put my hands out. She laughed and took them, hoisting herself up.

"Where?" she asked.

"Ice cream."

"Why?" She laughed, shaking her head.

"Since when do you need a reason to have ice cream?"

She nodded. "Okay, let's go then."

***

My jaw tensed when I saw the incoming number. I glanced over at Beth, who was still busy ordering ice cream.

"Hello?" I said, keeping my voice low.

"Roman. I was beginning to think you might've fled the country. You're a hard man to get a hold of."

"I'm a busy man. How can I help you?" I replied, my

tone cool.

"I'm hoping you have some information for me. You do remember our deal, don't you? If you'd rather just hand over the cash you owe me, that's fine, too." Yeah, right. Like I had a choice.

"I don't know what you want me to say. I'm doing what you asked."

"Are you? Because from what I hear, you're doing more than what I asked of you. I hired you because I thought you were responsible enough to not hit on her, Roman. Or at least desperate enough for the cash."

"What do you need?"

"I need information, Roman. My client is getting antsy. He is paying big bucks to know everything there is to know about this girl."

"And how do I know this information is not going to be abused?" I retorted. I ran a hand through my hair, trying to keep my frustration under control.

"That's really none of your business, is it?"

"Look, I'm with her now. I have to go. I will call you later." I hung up as Beth walked back over to me with two heavily scooped cups of ice cream.

"Everything all right?" she asked, handing me a cup.

"Yes, fine. Mint choc-chip. Good choice," I said, changing the subject. I turned quickly, running into someone. "Sorry—" I started, looking up. *Oh, shit.*

Dahlia's mouth broke into a smile. "Roman." Then she spotted Beth. Her eyes widened, then she turned back to me and winked. God only knows what she was thinking. Andrew stood behind Dahlia awkwardly, like he wasn't sure whether to acknowledge me or not.

"Dahlia. Andrew." I nodded. "This is my friend, Beth. Beth, these are some old friends of mine."

Beth smiled and held out her hand. "Lovely to meet you," she grinned.

"So, are you Roman's girlfriend?" Dahlia asked, her voice curious. She looked from Beth to me. I knew exactly what she was thinking: *When are you bringing her to the club?*

"Just good friends, Dahlia. We better let you two get going. You don't want to miss your movie," I said pointedly, praying she would take the hint.

"What...oh, yes. The movie." She raised her eyebrows at me and led Andrew away. I sighed, my heart pounding at the close call that had been. In all my time at the club, that was the first time I had ever run into any of its members.

That had been way, way too close.

Chapter Twenty

Beth

"So, how long have you known them?"

"Not that long."

"How did you meet?" I pressed.

Roman was quiet for a moment. "We met through other friends. We catch up once a month for dinner and a few drinks." He hesitated. What wasn't he telling me?

"You seem . . . I don't know. You're so mysterious. I feel like I never know if you're telling me the complete truth."

"Some things don't need to be told, Beth." He held my gaze and gave me a small smile.

Which only left me wondering, what wasn't he telling me?

Chapter Twenty-One

Beth

Things were going so well. I was very slowly
beginning to feel like myself again. I could almost forget
what had happened if I didn't have to see Ivan almost every
day. And Roman was . . . well, Roman. What could I say?
He was amazing. Things were finally going right for me.

I was expecting Roman to arrive any minute when my
phone began to ring. I checked the caller ID and nearly
fainted. It was Coop. Coop was calling me. My heart began
to pound.

Do I answer?

I clicked answer and held the phone to my ear, frozen.

"Beth?"

I closed my eyes, his voice melting through me. God, I'd missed that sound.

"Hi," I managed. I was in shock that I'd actually answered, and I think he was too. We had been emailing for a while, and texting—but talking? This was a big step for me.

I sat down on the sofa, telling myself to breathe.

"How are you? It's so good to hear your voice," he said.

You too. God, I've missed you so much.

"It's good to hear yours too. How's your mom?" Yes, I headed right for the safe topic. I was still paying for her treatment at the clinic. During all that had happened, it never once crossed my mind to pull the funding. I'd never do that to him.

"She's good. Some days are better than others, but she hasn't really gotten worse."

"That's great," I said, my voice soft. I closed my eyes.

My heart ached. Was I over him? No. Had I forgiven him? I was trying my damn hardest. I blinked back tears as the intercom buzzed.

Roman had arrived.

"Coop, I have to go." I hesitated. "It was great talking to you."

"You too, Beth. I love you."

But not in the way I longed for you to love me.

Hanging up the phone, I buzzed Roman in and met him at the door. I nearly melted on the spot. *Does this guy get sexier every time I see him?*

I took in his black pants and charcoal pinstriped shirt, which was open at the collar. He smiled that sexy, heart-fluttering smile and I sighed. I could stare at him all day. What struck me as surprising was how quickly Coop had escaped my thoughts.

I opened the door and walked back into the kitchen, knowing he was right behind me. This had become a pattern. He was here every night. Or I was at his place. I'd cooked extra tonight, knowing he was going to be coming over. How fucked up was that? And the fact that I was cooking? Even more fucked up, considering how bad my cooking skills were. I could burn water.

"You're no longer surprised at me turning up. Maybe I need to switch up my game," he joked, slipping his arms around my waist.

I turned around and reached up to kiss him. "I'm not surprised because you do whatever you want. I don't think anything would surprise me anymore."

He raised an eyebrow but said nothing as he took off his jacket. Again, he was in a suit.

"What do you do, anyway?"

"Pardon?"

"For work. You're always so nicely dressed." Every day he was in a suit, and it had just struck me that I had no idea what he did. I suspected something boring, like tax or law.

He laughed. "There's something wrong with a guy

who always likes to look his best? You never know who's watching, Beth."

"I guess not." I grimaced, thinking back on the number of times I'd dashed out of the house with no makeup and in my grungiest sweatpants. "But that didn't answer my question."

"I'm a businessman."

I rolled my eyes. *Very informative.*

"Okay, but what is it you do?" Every time I broached the subject of his career, he switched the conversation into another direction. It always worked too.

He sighed and moved toward me. Now he was making me nervous. What could be that big a deal that he couldn't tell me?

"I own a club."

"A club? What, like a bar?" I asked, confused. That was the big deal?

He chuckled and wiped his mouth. "Not exactly. My club is catered toward a specific clientele." He hesitated, turning to face me. "I own an exclusive erotic establishment."

"You mean a strip club?" I replied.

He laughed. "God, no. My club is where people who are looking to fulfill a fantasy can go to meet like-minded individuals."

"You sound like a late night TV commercial," I muttered, stabbing at the sauce. "How long have you had this club?"

"A few years. Beth, when you're ready, I'll tell you everything you want to know. You want to go there? Fine, I'm more than happy to take you."

"Fine, dinner is ready anyway," I announced proudly. *Although I don't know how proud I'll be once he tastes my cooking.*

"Good, I'm ravenous. What's on the menu?"

"We have chicken and avocado pasta, with a side of garlic bread."

"Mmm," he said, wrapping his arms around me. "And

for dessert?" he asked, raising an eyebrow.

I leaned up and kissed him tenderly. "You'll have to wait and see."

I walked back into the kitchen, swinging my hips as I walked, well aware that he was probably checking out my ass.

"You can pour the wine this time."

He laughed and went to the fridge. "How is your hand?"

I held it up proudly, the wound completely healed.

"Very good," he mumbled, reaching for my hand and kissing it. He set the bottle down and continued kissing along my arm, his dark eyes full of want. I shivered as his lips moved along my collarbone and up my neck. The way his tongue was drawing circles on my skin was making me wet.

"Dinner is going to burn," I mumbled, his lips finding mine.

"So turn it off," he whispered. His hands moved

underneath my dress.

Wrapping my arms around his neck, I kissed him, passion overtaking my hunger. The only thing I wanted right then was him.

My arm flailing behind me, I switched off the burner. He lifted me onto his hips, his mouth never breaking from mine. This was incredible. Everything about him made me feel safe…and loved. Even though we hadn't gone there, I could feel it.

I took him by the hand to stroke the tender skin underneath my shirt, my eyes never leaving his. I gave him a small smile, because words were unnecessary. He knew.

"Are you sure?" he asked, stroking my face.

I nodded. I was ready for this, and more than that, I needed this. He led me into the bedroom. He knelt before me, his touch caressing the fabric of my panties; his gentle kisses to my pubic bone left a numbing sensation in their wake. Giving me a nod and blinking slowly, he eased them down over my knees, letting them fall to my feet.

Dressed in only my shirt, I watched as he undid each

button, one by one, his eyes never leaving mine. I breathed in deeply as his hands slipped the shirt over my shoulders until I stood naked in front of him. I watched him take his shirt off, then his pants.

"You're so beautiful," he whispered as his fingers trailed from above my breasts down through the middle until they reached the beginning of my sex. I closed my eyes as his fingers slowly trailed up and down. I was so wet. My knees buckled as he slid a finger inside me.

With his other hand cupping my face, he brought me closer to him until our bodies pressed flush up against one another. His lips connected with mine, our mouths moving as one in such an intimate, personal way.

Tilting my head back, I sighed as he slipped a second finger inside of me. I couldn't describe how amazing it felt. It was like he knew exactly what I needed, what my body craved.

He gently lay me down on the bed, his fingers still circling inside me. I moved my legs further apart, willing them to plunge deeper inside of me. He kissed my neck, his tongue drawing softly along my collarbone. I was in heaven. This was the single most intimate experience of my life.

I moaned, stroking my nipples as he nibbled on my ear, his tongue curling around my lobe.

"Please, I need you," I whispered, wanting him inside me. I reached down, wrapping my fingers around his erection, gently stroking back and forth. He reached for the condom on the bedside table, rolling it on.

Poised at my entrance, he stared into my eyes as he pushed himself inside me, creating a slow and steady rhythm of rocking back and forth. I closed my eyes and sighed, the connection I felt with him unlike anything else.

"Are you okay?" he asked.

I nodded, curling my legs around his waist. His thrusts deepened and increased in speed as the climax began to build in both of us. He groaned as he released inside me, his eyes never straying from mine.

He kissed me, his fingers stroking my hair.

"I love you, Beth," he said, his voice hoarse.

My eyes widened. I kissed him again, this time with more passion and more desire.

"I love you too."

Chapter Twenty-Two

Beth

The knock caught me off guard. Roman was early. I quickly tidied up the kitchen and then raced for the door, my excitement to see him surprising even me. I swung open the door, unable to wipe the smile off my face. *Wow, I have energy. Where the hell did that come from?*

My face froze when I realized it wasn't Roman, but Ivan standing there.

"What do you want?" I asked in a shrill voice, trying to push the door closed. But before I could close it, his foot wedged its way in between the door and the frame.

"Come on, Bethy, is that anyway to speak to the man who gave you your dreams?" Sarcasm. Great. I fell backward as he pushed his way inside.

"Get out, Ivan. I mean it. Now." All I could think was that I wished I felt as strong as I sounded right then.

"Settle down, I'm here on business only." He sighed. "You're going to L.A. next week for a read-through for the part. I need you to deliver something for me."

"What?" I said, confused. *I haven't even agreed to try out yet, and all of a sudden I have an audition?* I loved the idea of acting, sure, but I hated him presuming I would say yes. Part of me wanted to turn it down just to spite him. "You can't run my life, Ivan. You don't get to decide what I do."

His eyes narrowed as he stepped toward me, a cocky expression on his face. "I got the feeling you couldn't wait to get away from me for a while, Bethy." He reached out and fingered my dress.

I stood there, terrified and unable to move. Just like that, I was back to that night. I'd never be free from him. He was always going to have this over me. "You just remember, honey, last time? That was nothing compared to what I'm capable of. I *own* you." His mouth was inches from mine, his eyes burning into me, into my soul. My knees weakened, and I struggled to keep my composure.

"Leave me *alone*," I hissed. "Get the fuck out, and leave me the hell alone. I have a friend who will be here any moment, and if he sees you, I guarantee you'll be sorry."

He laughed, but backed off. "Don't threaten me, Bethy. You have no idea who you're dealing with. I'll be in touch."

***

A suspicious-looking package arrived three days later via Ivan's personal courier. The small, well-wrapped parcel was heavy and solid. My heart sank as I tried to convince myself that it wasn't what I thought it was.

I set it down in front of me and carefully unwrapped the brown paper that covered it. Sighing, I sat back and stared at the clear package of white powder sitting in front of me. There had to be more than two pounds of coke here. What the hell was I? A drug courier now? No fucking way. I'd rather lose everything than do this.

Fuck Ivan.

How much more could he fuck my life up than he already had? There was nothing he could do to me that would hurt me more than he already had. This was my chance to hurt *him*. I wanted him to suffer just as he had done to me.

I swiftly picked up the package and my phone, and headed to the bathroom. Before I could second guess what I was doing, I'd slashed the top of the package open and was pouring the contents into the toilet, all the while filming it with my other hand. I coughed as the residue from the substance filled the air.

"See that, Ivan? That is what I think of you. Go to hell, you fucking fuck." I spat out the words with venom. I pressed stop, and then sent the video to his cell.

It took less than a minute for my phone to start ringing. I stared at it in shock.

Holy shit, what have I done?

My heart began to race as I processed what had happened. What was the street value of coke these days?

How much cash had I just flushed down the toilet? More to the point, who owned that coke?

My phone continued to ring nonstop. I didn't answer, even though I knew he was probably on his way over. I paced the hallway, panicking. What the hell was I going to do? I reached for my phone and called Roman.

"Hey," he said warmly.

"I'm in trouble," I blurted out.

"What's wrong?" he asked, immediately concerned. "Are you okay?"

"No," I sobbed. "God, I did something really stupid . . ." I burst into tears and collapsed onto the floor. All I'd wanted to do was to get Ivan off my back.

"I'm on my way. It will be okay, Beth, try not to worry."

***

I waited for what felt like hours for Roman to arrive. In reality, it was only a few minutes. As I stood by the door waiting to spot his car, my phone beeped. My hands shook as I read the message.

You stupid little bitch. Do you have any idea what you've done? If you think I was rough with you, these guys will make our time together seem like a sweet teenage romance. These guys have killed for less than this, Beth.

I was hysterical.

How could I have been so stupid? I'd wanted to hurt him like he hurt me—only all I'd done was gotten myself into a whole heap of shit. I'd been around enough drug dealers to know that they didn't mess around. When they found out what I'd done, they'd hunt me down and kill me. Or worse.

Sliding down the wall, I sat on the floor, hugging my knees to my chest, panicking and silently freaking out. *Please hurry. Come on, Roman. Hurry.*

Chapter Twenty-Three

Roman

The ten-minute drive to her place seemed to take hours. I hadn't felt this nervous in years. She could barely speak on the phone; something was seriously wrong, and I had no idea what that was.

Finally, her place came into view. I slammed my foot on the accelerator and drove up the hill, screeching into her driveway. The gate was open. Why was the gate open? The gate was never open. Beth was one of the most security-conscious people I'd ever met.

Blood pounded through my body as I climbed out of my car and ran to the door.

"Beth? It's Roman. Let me in." The door opened,

revealing a terrified-looking Beth standing behind it. She was literally shaking like a leaf, her eyes wide with fear. I walked in and took her in my arms. She burst into tears, relaxing into my embrace.

I walked her over to the sofa and sat her down. I needed her to calm down if I was going to find out what the hell was wrong. So help me God, if anyone had hurt her . . . Let's just say things wouldn't end well for them.

"Beth, I need you to calm down. Look at me, Beth. Look at me."

She lifted her eyes to mine. What the hell had her so terrified? She was shaking, and her face was white except for her eyes, which were red from crying. Even in this state, she was the most beautiful creature I'd ever seen.

"I can't," she whispered.

"Beth, you can. You're one of the strongest people I've ever met. You can do whatever you want to do. Tell me what happened. Tell me what's wrong so I can fix it."

"You can't fix this, Roman."

"Let me try. Did someone hurt you?"

Her sobs got louder. And there was my answer. My body tensed at the thought of anyone laying a finger on her. Shit. I'd fucking kill the bastard.

"Beth, I need you to talk to me, okay? I'm two seconds away from calling the cops."

Her head shot up. Her eyes were wide with fear. "Don't do that! Please, *please* don't do that."

"Then you'd better tell me what the hell is going on."

"I did something. I did something really stupid."

"What? What did you do, Beth?"

"I'm in some serious trouble. I can't stay here," she declared. She jumped up, glancing around the room, that same look of terror in her eyes. "They know where I live. This is the first place they'll look. I've got to go."

I followed her as she ran toward her bedroom. I watched as she grabbed a bag and begun stuffing random items of clothing into it.

"Fine, come with me, you can tell me what the hell this is all about on the way."

"Roman, no. This is my mess, not yours. I don't want or need your help."

I snorted and reached out, grabbing hold of her hand. "Then why did you call me? You know what, Beth? It kind of looks like you *do* need my help."

Without a word, I walked her outside and opened the passenger door, waiting for her to get in.

She glared at me and stood her ground, as if she had some kind of point to prove. "I don't need you to save me."

"Beth, get in the fucking car. If things are as bad as you say they are, then every second you stand here and argue is one second you're closer to having to explain yourself to *them* rather than me." I shrugged as if I didn't care. "Your choice."

That got her attention. Her pretty face creased into a frown as she crouched down into the passenger seat, scowling.

Sighing, I slammed the door and walked around to the driver's side. "So, are you going to tell me what is going on?"

She didn't respond. Instead, she just stared out the window. I glanced down at her fingers, which were fidgeting like crazy in her lap. I sighed. What did I have to do here? I was so worried about her, but if she wouldn't tell me what was wrong, I couldn't help her.

We drove in silence, and I figured the best thing I could do right then was wait until she was ready to talk. Whatever was wrong, at least I could protect her if she was with me.

I drove us out through the mountains to a small fishing shack my father used to own. I was about ninety percent sure it was abandoned, so I figured it was as good a place as any to hide out for a few days. As we drove through the last town before the shack, I stopped to grab some supplies.

"You stay here. Do you need anything?"

She shook her head. Nodding, I climbed out of the car and slammed the door. She was so damned frustrating sometimes.

I put her out of my mind as I walked around the supermarket, grabbing handfuls of supplies—enough to last us a few days. Until I knew what the hell was wrong, I had no real plan in mind of what to do. I mean, for all I knew she could be in the shit for missing a day at work. I chuckled to myself. Maybe this was her way of trying to get me alone? No—if Beth was one thing, it was forward. She didn't hide behind games. If she wanted me alone, she would just ask.

I walked back to the car and threw the bag of groceries in the trunk.

"You sure you don't want a bathroom break or anything?" I asked her, my voice soft.

She half-smiled and shook her head. "I'm okay," she mumbled.

She speaks! At least we were getting somewhere.

"The cabin's not too far away. We will be safe there for a few days, but I am going to need to know what's going on."

She nodded and looked away.

I pulled up outside the old wooden shack, where I had spent many weekends as a child. It looked abandoned. Well, more than that that, it looked unsafe for human habitation. The roof toward the back of the shack had begun to cave in. The once bright yellow paint had peeled off, revealing the rotted weatherboards. Every window had been smashed. God, even the door was barely hanging on by a hinge. But I had to make the best of the situation. I caught Beth eyeing the cabin dubiously, which made me smile.

This place was definitely a step down for the princess.

"Can you handle a couple of days roughing it?" I smirked.

She shot me a *look*, her eyes narrowing. "Can you?" she retorted.

Fair point.

Chapter Twenty-Four

Roman

"Beth, I need you to tell me what is going on. I want to help you, but I don't know how."

She sat on the sofa, with me kneeling between her legs, my hands resting on her thighs.

I reached up and tilted her chin. Her sad eyes gazed back at me. "Please, talk to me."

"I did something really stupid," she whispered. Her face was drained of color, as if she'd just realized the full ramifications of her actions. She was beginning to scare me. What the hell could she have done that was so bad? She was terrified.

"Tell me what you did, Beth."

She closed her eyes and took a deep breath. "There was a package. It . . . it was cocaine. A block of coke wrapped in plastic. Ivan wanted me to deliver it to someone in L.A. next week."

"Where is it now?"

"In the toilet," she sobbed.

I looked at her. What? She was crying so heavily I could barely understand her.

"Beth, I need you to look at me. I need you to calm down, okay?"

She nodded and took a deep breath. Her hands, cold and clammy, closed over mine.

"What do you mean it's in the toilet?"

"I was so angry at him. I wanted to hurt him, Roman. I wasn't thinking. I flushed it down the toilet. And filmed it. Then sent him the video."

Oh, shit. I racked my brain, trying to place this Ivan. I

was pretty sure she hadn't mentioned him before. "Who is Ivan?"

"My manager." Beth swallowed, blinking back her tears. "Ivan raped me. Nearly four months ago." She lowered her head, eyes closed, tears rolling down her cheeks.

My throat constricted as my mind processed what she'd just said. Surely I must've heard wrong?

"Ivan raped you." I sat forward, resting my elbows on my knees, anger rising inside of me. Her spiel about the assault being a year ago and not knowing him had been just to throw me off the trail. I wanted to break his fucking neck. "What happened, Beth? Did you tell anyone? Did you report it?" My voice was oddly calm, a complete contradiction to how I was feeling.

I was trying so damn hard to remain calm because I didn't want to upset her, but it was nearly impossible. I had to find him. I had to find him and kick the living shit out of him. I was going to kill the bastard.

"No." She shook her head.

Leaning forward, I pulled her in to me, wrapping my arms around her.

"I . . . there was nobody to tell. He threatened me. God, Roman, it was horrible. I was so scared."

"I can't believe you went through this alone," I murmured, holding her tight. I wanted to protect her. And I wanted to make him pay.

I swear on my life, that fucker is going to pay.

***

Beth lay on the bed when I entered the room, her eyes swollen and red. I zipped up my jacket, then leaned over her, kissing her tenderly.

"I'll be back soon, okay? Scarlett is here if you need anything. I promise I won't be long."

"Where are you going?" She sat up, terror in her wide eyes.

"I have to take care of something," I muttered, scowling.

"No! Please, Roman. Don't do anything stupid, please. *Please*."

"Beth, he has to pay. He needs to pay for what he did to you," I growled. "He's not going to get away with it."

"Please, just let it go," she begged. "I don't need you to fix things for me."

"No?" I said, my voice rising. "Who the *fuck* is going to do it if I don't, Beth?"

Chapter Twenty-Five

Beth

Pacing around the bedroom, I didn't know what to do. I was so worried about Roman, that he'd do something stupid or get himself hurt. I felt dizzy, sick, faint, and anxious: all the classic signs of a panic attack. Scarlett being there didn't make me feel any better. How was she going to protect me if Ivan found out where I was? She was tiny—smaller than me. She looked like she'd have trouble lifting a fork.

I grabbed my phone, my hands shaking like crazy. Punching in one of the few numbers I knew by heart, I waited for Coop to answer.

"Beth, what's wrong?" he asked.

I could hear the alarm in his voice. The words froze in my throat. All that would come out were sobs—loud, frantic sobs.

"Baby, you're scaring me. Where are you? Tell me where you are, and I'll come to you."

"I don't know. Some little cabin up on Forster Lake. Opposite the gas station," I added, remembering the abandoned complex just before we turned at the cabin. Dropping the phone, I curled up on the bed. Wrapping my arms around myself, I shivered. I was so cold. What if Roman got hurt? Ivan was dangerous. I knew that better than anyone. Or what if he killed Ivan? Or what if Ivan killed him?

The thought made me sick. Ivan had ruined my life enough. I didn't want to lose Roman because of him, too.

***

"Beth?" Scarlett knocked gently on the door. "Are you okay? Can I come in?"

"Yes."

She walked over and climbed onto the bed, curling her arms around me.

I exhaled, my hand gripping onto her wrist. "This is so messed up."

"It's not your fault. None of this is your fault."

I turned to face her. "You know, then?"

She nodded.

My lip quivered. All the progress I'd thought I was making was gone. I felt like I had right back in that moment: Powerless. Hopeless.

"Nobody should go through what you did alone." She stroked my arm. "And that bastard should pay for what he did. Roman's not stupid. You don't need to worry about him."

"Beth!"

A knock at the front door startled me. I sat up, relieved. Coop. He was here. Turning to Scarlett, I gave her a hug.

"Thanks for being here for me."

She smiled and hugged me back.

I stood up and raced for the door. I was so scared to see him again. The last time, at the restaurant, had not gone well. What if things felt awkward? I really needed a friend right now.

Taking a deep breath, I swung the door open. He threw his arms around me.

"God, Beth. I've been so fucking worried about you." He kissed my cheek as I hugged him back. The emotion I felt was relief. If things had been strained I don't think I could've handled it. "You look good."

"You too," I smiled. Fuck, I was almost in tears. I took his hand and led him inside. "Do you want a drink? A coffee?"

"Nah, I just had one not long ago." His eyes grew concerned. "What's wrong? Are you in trouble?"

I nodded. "Maybe a little." *God, where do I start?* "Coop, it's such a mess. I'm scared. I think he's going to kill him," I whispered.

"Who?"

"Ivan. Roman's gone after him."

"Ivan? What the hell—" He stopped and turned to me, his expression one of disbelief. "Did he hurt you?"

I began to cry. The whole story tumbled out in a flood of tears.

"Jesus, Beth, why the fuck didn't you tell me?"

"Because I was angry. I needed someone to blame and I…"

"You blamed me," he finished quietly.

"No! I was trapped in this never-ending nightmare. I needed to project the hurt and anger I was feeling somewhere, and I felt deserted by you since you met Mia." I took a deep breath, forcing myself to continue. "You canceled that night at the bar, and Ivan was there. He drove me home."

Coop's face went white. "*That's* when this happened?

Fuck, Beth, I'm so, so sorry."

"I don't blame you, Coop. *He* raped me, not you." I
threw my arms around him and wiped my damp cheeks.

"For what it's worth, I hope Roman fucks him up
really bad." He shook his head. "That fucking bastard."

.

The door opened, then slammed shut.

We both looked up as Roman walked into the room. I
edged slightly away from Coop. *I'm not sure why I did
that.* Roman stared at Coop, his expression hard. I
swallowed.

"Roman, this is an old friend of mine, Coop. Coop this
is…a new friend of mine, Roman." They stared each other
down, neither of them looking particularly pleased to see
the other. "How did it go?" I asked nervously.

"You don't need to worry about Ivan anymore."

I stared at him, waiting for him to elaborate. He didn't.
I watched as he walked out of the room.

"Wait," I said, getting to my feet. "What does that
mean?"

"It means he won't be bothering you again."

I shot Coop an apologetic look and ran after Roman. I had no idea what his problem was. I caught up with him and grabbed his arm. He turned around, his face softening.

"What happened? What do you mean I don't need to worry anymore? Did you…" I shuddered. I couldn't even bring myself to say it.

"Beth, just let it go. You can finally work on getting over what happened. What I said or did to him, it's better you don't know."

Well, that makes me feel better.

He sighed and took my hands in his. "He's not dead, if that's what you're worried about."

"Good." I placed his arms around my waist, and my own around his neck. "Thank you for not giving up on me. I still don't know why you were so insistent on helping me, but thank you." I lifted my mouth to his, our lips melding together. I felt him relax.

"Mmm. I could get used to this." He smiled, planting

another kiss on my lips.

"Ahem."

We both turned. I blushed. Shit. I'd forgotten about Coop. We all stood there awkwardly.

"I might go into town and get some food. Do you guys want anything?"

I shook my head, and so did Roman.

"Okay, I'll check into my hotel too. If it's okay, I'll come over later?"

I glanced at Roman, who shrugged.

"Sure," he said.

I squeezed his hand and smiled at him, appreciating the effort he was making.

"Hey, why don't you stay here? There's a spare bedroom. Doesn't make sense for you to be staying in a hotel," he said gruffly.

Wow. I glanced at Roman, a huge smile on my face. I

was so proud of him.

"Thanks." Coop met my eye. "I'll do that."

Chapter Twenty-Six

Beth

"You seem really happy."

I smiled at Coop. "I guess I am."

"I'm glad, Beth. I'm so sorry I wasn't there for you. Every time I think about how hard it must have been for you going through that alone..." He stopped and shook his head.

We sat on the beach a short walk from the shack. Roman refused to let me leave until he had sorted out the coke money. Not that I wanted to go anywhere just yet. The thought of the bad guys coming after me... I shuddered.

Roman knew someone who could track down the guys

who owned the drugs. Ivan had given up their names in exchange for keeping his balls, according to Roman.

I kind of wished he hadn't.

"I wanted to say to you that I'm sorry for ignoring your calls and texts for so long," I said, reaching for Coop's hand.

He turned to me in shock. "Are you serious? Beth, I don't blame you for one second. I'm just glad I didn't give up on you."

"I'm glad too," I mumbled. I hugged him. "So, how are you? How's Mia? Are you still studying?"

"Yep, still studying. I'm liking it, but it's much harder than I was expecting."

"And Mia?" I asked again. Why did I feel nervous all of a sudden?

"Mia is good," he finally said. "We've had our problems, but we're getting there."

I nodded. Was I the cause of their problems? Coop had spent so much of the last couple of months consumed with me…I wasn't sure how I felt about that. I was over Coop. Wasn't I?

Yes. You're with Roman now.

"Mia is a good girl, Coop. Don't lose her, okay?" I said carefully.

"I don't know anymore, Beth. The last two months, all I've thought about is you. Not having you in my life…" He shook his head and stared at the sand.

"I'm happy, Coop. Roman makes me feel alive."

"And I didn't?" he asked.

I swallowed hard. *Please don't ask me this.* "I'm not the same person I was back then. Everything that's happened, I've changed so much."

"I just want the chance to get to know you again, then, Beth. I don't want to lose our friendship. You mean too much to me."

I reached out and hugged him, kissing his neck. It felt good to have my friend back.

Chapter Twenty-Seven

Roman

This is not a good idea.

I glanced down the alley on either side of me. At nearly three a.m., the place was deserted.

My heart was sitting in my throat as I picked the lock of the garage that doubled as Carlos's haunt.

Three hours of scoping the place out, and he had finally left. Who goes out at three a.m.? Not that I cared. I needed him gone so I could get answers.

The lock broke free, and I pushed my way inside. I'd been there often enough to know the positioning of the cameras. There were no alarms to worry about—only

Skippy. Speaking of which . . .

"Come here boy," I muttered, kneeling down. The ninety-pound Doberman bounded toward me, his tail wagging, tongue hanging out everywhere. He lapped at my face happily. I laughed. *Worst guard dog ever.* I petted him for a good few minutes, and then got my mission back on track.

Pointing my flashlight down the hall, I made my way into Carlos's office, Skippy right behind me, bouncing around excitedly like he was on crack. I shook my head as he stared up at me with his huge brown eyes.

Glancing quickly around the office, I tried to form a plan of attack. I'd meticulously organized getting myself in here, but had little plan in mind for what to do once that actually happened.

I guessed the desk was as good a place as any to start.

What was I looking for? Anything that would tell me who had hired Carlos. The last thing Beth needed was any more surprises. I had no idea what this person wanted from her, but I was going to protect her, even if it meant breaking the law to do it.

Sitting at the desk, I switched on the lamp and began shuffling through each drawer. Nothing really stood out: papers, work receipts, the odd porn magazine . . . Carlos wasn't stupid enough to leave anything incriminating just lying around, but I'd hoped he might've been a bit careless when rushing out in the middle of the night.

As I stood up, something caught my eye. My brow furrowed as I reached for a framed photo that sat proudly on the corner of his desk.

No fucking way.

I had seen this picture before—in Beth's box of her childhood memories. Only in this photo Carlos was holding her, smiling as she giggled. She looked about two, maybe younger, tiny blonde curls clinging to her head.

I couldn't believe this. How had I not figured this out earlier? Carlos was Beth's father. I was *sure* of it. The only proof I had was this photo, though, and the feeling in my gut. What the hell did he want from her? Was he after money? I snorted. Carlos was always after money.

***

A million scenarios ran through my head, and none of them were good. I wanted answers, and I wasn't leaving until I got them. I didn't care if I was waiting there all fucking night: Carlos was going to tell me everything, or I would beat him to a pulp.

It turned out I didn't have to wait long. Fifteen minutes later, he walked through the door clutching a bag of takeout. Spotting me, he whipped a gun out of his pocket and aimed it at me. I snorted. What, he was going to shoot me?

"What the fuck are you doing here?" Carlos snarled as he glared at me. He lowered the gun and glanced at Skippy, curled up by my feet, snoring away. "Fucking useless mutt."

I tapped my fingers on the desk and stared at the photo I was still holding in my hand. His eyes darted toward it, then back to me as he realized I knew.

"It's none of your business, Roman. I'm paying you for a job—that's it. None of this concerns you," he said defensively.

"But it does," I said, standing up. "It became my

282

concern the day you asked me to watch her." I walked around to the front of the desk and leaned against it. "What do you want with her? Money? She's been through enough without you fucking up her life even more." The words tumbled out of me, harsh and cold.

He dropped the gun onto the table and sat down. His face grew tired as he sat there, looking defeated. "I'm not after her money, Roman. I don't want anything from her."

"Then why all this? Why pay me to watch her?" I asked, shaking my head. It didn't make sense.

"I've been watching her for years. Since her mother kicked me out when she was two. Every step she made, I was there, watching."

"Why wouldn't you just tell her? Why hide from her?" I didn't get it. If he had been watching her, he would've known exactly what she'd been through. What kind of father would just stand back and let her cope with that alone?

"Come on, Roman. Look at me. I'm a petty criminal. Hell, I should be in prison for some of the things I've done. Do you really think she needed someone like me in her life? Her mother wouldn't let me anywhere near her. Then when she went to live with Kayla, I figured she'd be better off there."

"And when Kayla died?" I challenged.

He shrugged. "She was still a hell of a lot better alone than with me. Look at her. She's a superstar. All I would have done is messed up her life. She didn't need me."

"She needed *someone*," I roared. Blood pulsated through my veins. "Do you have any idea what she's been through? Why did you hire me? Did you know about Ivan?"

"Ivan? Ivan is a piece of scum. I never trusted him." Carlos narrowed his eyes. "Wait, what do you mean? What are you talking about, Ivan?" He took a step forward. "Did he hurt her?"

"He raped her. He raped her, then threatened her, and now she's mixed up in something really bad because she doesn't think before she acts."

"I'll kill the son of a bitch," he cursed. "That fucking good-for-nothing piece of shit. He's gonna pay. Where the hell is he?"

I put my hands up and shook my head. "Trust me, he's not going anywhere for a few days. I may have lost my temper."

"I don't give a flying fuck! I want to kill the bastard," he seethed, wrapping his hands behind his head. "Fucking fuck-knuckled shithead. Nobody lays a finger on my daughter and lives to gloat about it."

"Carlos, don't do anything stupid, okay?" I sighed. Not that I could talk; I'd been as angry as him when I'd found out.

"What, like slice his fucking dick off?" Carlos growled. "I'm not stupid, Roman. I can look after myself and my family."

I groaned. Great, so now she was family. I slapped a piece of paper down on his desk.

"What's this?" he asked, picking it up.

"That is the owner of the ten pounds of coke Beth flushed down the toilet."

"She what?" Carlos sputtered, roaring with laughter. "That's my kid, all right."

I frowned. "She is happy to pay for what she damaged, but can you take care of this? I don't want her to have to deal with anything else."

"Yeah. Leave it with me." He stood up, leaning over his desk until he was nose to nose with me. "You fucking hurt a single hair on her head and I'll rip your balls off, stick 'em in a blender, and pour them down your throat. Got it?" He glared at me menacingly.

"Got it, Carlos." I shook my head and walked out.

Chapter Twenty-Eight

Roman

"Tickets?" I asked.

She held up our two first-class tickets.

"Okay, then. I guess that's it." I picked up the last of our luggage and carried it out to the waiting cab.

Getting the role in the movie could not have come at a more perfect time. Even though she had missed her audition and now had no manager, they had been so keen to secure her for the part, they'd offered her a deal she couldn't pass up.

After the last few months, we both needed to get away for a while—and it was only for six months. To be honest, I couldn't wait to start my life with Beth. I fell asleep thinking about her and woke up wanting her. She was truly the most amazing woman I'd ever met, and I still struggled to comprehend that she chose me. Out of all the men in the world, I'm the one she wanted.

I'd left Scarlett in charge at the club. She had been shocked when I'd asked her, but it hadn't taken much to convince her that she was up for it. Strangely enough, without the debts hanging over my head, I actually felt really relaxed about leaving my baby in her hands.

Carlos had surprised me with his restraint in dealing with Ivan . . . if you call planting ten pounds of coke in his home, tipping off the cops, and getting him thrown in jail being restrained. Ivan had pleaded guilty and received six years.

Six years was nothing compared to what he'd put Beth through. He would get his life back in six years; she would remember that night forever.

"So, I guess we are really doing this, huh?" Beth asked, linking her arm in mine.

"Guess so." I cradled her face in my hand as I kissed her, not caring that we had an audience in the middle-aged driver who was watching us in the rearview mirror.

Beth giggled.

My phone beeped. Pulling it out of my pocket, I recognized the number as Carlos's.

I told you I'd take care of him

At first I thought he was referring to planting the drugs. Then I saw the link at the bottom of the text. I clicked on it.

A fifty-six-year-old prisoner serving time for drug possession and distribution charges has been left paralyzed and brain damaged after a vicious attack. The apparently unprovoked assault occurred during exercise time Monday morning.

The prisoner suffered major internal injuries after being sodomized with an iron bar and beaten to near death.

Prison officials are holding two inmates on suspicion of committing the assault, both of whom are already serving life sentences for murder convictions.

Holy fuck. I glanced at Beth, who was gazing happily out the window. She didn't need to hear this right now.

She was happier than I'd seen her in months—too happy for me to tell her this news right now, and too happy for me to tell her the truth about how we met. The only people who knew that were Scarlett, Carlos, and I. Telling Beth wouldn't change the way I felt about her, or what had happened between us.

She had been through enough. I knew I could make her happy. I was going to make her happy. I could care for her better than anyone else ever could.

And maybe one day, I'd be able to share all my secrets with her.

Epilogue

Beth

"Glad to be home?" Roman came up behind me and wrapped his arms around my waist.

I smiled, turning my head to kiss his cheek. "I am. But home is anywhere you are."

After wrapping up the movie, we were back home in New York. Things were going really well. Roman had been just amazing. He had been my rock. There was not a thing he could do wrong. I'd been so hesitant to let another man into my heart, but he'd just refused to give up on me.

I'd kept in contact with Coop—we spoke a few times a week, and our friendship was stronger than ever. Sometimes I got the feeling that he might've wanted something more between us, but I was happy the way things were. Maybe I was still in love with Coop, but the love I felt for Roman was so effortless, and I just knew he would always be there for me.

Acting had been surprisingly enjoyable—much more so than singing. I had a new manager, a middle-aged woman known as 'the shark.' As tough as she was, I felt completely at ease around her—something I'd never felt with Ivan.

Ivan. When I heard what had happened to him in prison, I was happy. It seemed deserved. I never thought I'd wish harm on another human being, but that was before…I was a different person now. A stronger one. I could handle anything.

Roman

It didn't get any better than this. I gazed down at Beth, wrapped in my arms, and smiled. I was so proud of her, and the way she had handled herself. She had even been seeing a counselor back in L.A.

I finally felt like we were moving forward. Nobody knows what the future holds, so it was pointless worrying about it. I had secrets—plenty of them. If Beth ever found out some of the things I'd kept hidden…that was something I didn't want to think about.

Did I regret accepting Carlos' job offer? No, because had it not been for him, I never would have met her. My only regret was not telling her the moment I started falling in love with her, because now, this had to stay buried.

She would never find out. I'd make sure of it.

*Book three in the Tease series, **Scandalous**, will be released mid 2014*

See over the page for Chapter One of Scandalous

Scandalous

Chapter One

Beth

"You sure about this?"

I nodded, my fingers entwining in his. I'd been hinting to Roman that I wanted to see his club. The way he explained it to me—sex, adventure, pushing the boundaries while *you* are in control—how could that *not* appeal to me?

Still, I couldn't shake the feeling that I had no idea what I was getting myself into. He pulled up in front of the entrance, where a man in a suit stood, waiting to take the car. From the outside, it looked like just another factory. Dirty and dark, it resembled something out of a horror movie. You would never suspect what took place inside.

"Does it make you aroused? Having me come here?" I asked, a smile spreading across my lips.

"I guess you could say that." He chuckled as he opened the front door. "Are you ready?" he asked, his voice husky. I nodded, pushing aside my uneasiness. The last time I'd felt this nervous, things had gone badly.

I scanned the room, unsure of where to look first. People stood in clusters, chatting, laughing, and drinking. There could've only been forty people, max. All were dressed elegantly in cocktail dresses and suits. This place had much more class than I was expecting. There were no strippers dancing on poles, or naked women serving alcohol—just everyday people. People like me. I glanced at Roman, who squeezed my hand.

"I won't leave you, and the second you feel uncomfortable, we're out of here." He spoke in a soft voice, his eyes searching mine for reassurance that I was okay.

I nodded, not wanting to let on just how exciting I found all of this. Not yet, anyway.

Roman led me over to the bar. His arm slipped around my back, holding me close. I took the opportunity to take in my surroundings. The place was huge, with a large space that at first glance could be mistaken for a dance floor. The walls were lined with plush red sofas where people sat, nursing drinks and interacting.

"So everyone here is a participant?" I was still having trouble grasping the concept. It wasn't a brothel…but people had sex?

"Not the staff. The staff can participate, but not while they are working. Everyone is here willingly, and we have plenty of measures in place to ensure nothing gets out of hand." He pointed behind us. "See over there?"

I looked at what appeared to be giant glass boxes. Roman laughed.

"They are the private rooms."

"They don't look very private," I muttered. He chuckled and took my hand, leading me in that direction.

"Sit down here," he said as we stopped outside one of the 'rooms.'

I gawked at him. "But there is a couple in there! I'm sure they don't want us watching them…" He sat down, pulling me onto his lap. I gasped and glared at him. He was hard!

"Beth, people come here to be watched. Look at them."

I did as he said and turned my attention to the couple. The chick was stunning. She leaned naked against the bed, her knee bent and her foot resting on her partner's shoulder. He kneeled between her legs, his tongue buried deep inside her.

This is so naughty.

As if she heard me, she opened her eyes and stared directly at me as she gripped the back of his head. Her chin tilted up as her body began to convulse, her eyes still on mine.

Holy fuck.

I heard the sound of Roman's zipper as he guided my hand behind my back and curled my fingers around his hard cock. I worked my fingers into a rhythm, moving up and down his shaft.

He expertly maneuvered my panties down and flipped up the back of my dress. I gasped, closing my eyes as he lifted me onto his tip. Slowly, he thrust inside me, his hands on my hips.

Glancing back at the couple, I saw the man stand behind as he drove himself inside her. She bit her lip and groaned, making eye contact with me. Her eyes narrowed and her lips lifted into a smile.

Roman's hand moved down the top of my dress as he massaged my breast. I couldn't believe how turned on I was just then. It was unlike anything I'd ever experienced.

Reaching to the side of my strapless dress, I shrugged it down, exposing my breasts. Roman groaned and kissed my neck, his hands moving rapidly over my breasts as he began to ride me faster.

"Oh god," I whispered, tweaking my nipple. I lowered my hand between my legs and began to rub myself. *Oh shit, yes, fuck!*

"I'm nearly there babe," he whispered, his tongue swirling behind my ear. "Fuck, you feel so good," he groaned, pumping his hips into mine. "Yeahhh…."

My fingers worked inside me alongside him as I began to climax. Both the man and the woman were watching me now, obviously enjoying the show. I cried out, falling back against Roman as his fingers trailed down to my wetness, easing the last few moments of my climax from me.

"Wow." I exhaled, exhausted. And hot. I wiped away the moisture from the back of my neck and repositioned my dress. As I stood up, Roman eased himself out of me and tucked himself back in.

"I'm surprised, Beth," he murmured as we walked back over to the bar. "I didn't expect that."

Neither had I. Being watched…and watching…wow, I couldn't string words together to give the pleasure I was feeling justice. I glanced around the room and smiled. How this place had stayed such a secret was beyond me. But if there was one thing I knew better than anyone, it was that secrets don't stay secrets for long.

And sometimes when they broke, they became scandalous.

A Note From The Author

If you or someone you know has experienced a sexual assault, it is important to know you are not alone. There are many centers, some with 24-hour hotlines with experienced counselors, who can help you and offer you assistance.

U.S.
National Sexual Assault Hotline 1-800-656-HOPE

U.K.
Rape Crisis 0808 802 9999

AUSTRALIA
Sexual Assault & Domestic Violence Hotline 1800 RESPECT (1800 737 732)

INTERNATIONAL RESOURCES
RAINN   http://www.rainn.org/get-help/sexual-assault-and-rape-international-resources

Bad Boy Rockers series, by Lexi Buchanan

Book One: Sizzle ~ Out now at all major online retailers
Book Two: Spicy ~ Out now at all major online retailers

Sizzle Synopsis

*****This book is erotica.*****

Because of screwing up with Callie, during the summer, I'm drowning my sorrows with drink and women…or that's what I'm trying to do, but it isn't working. Every time I close my eyes all I see is Callie, her long flowing blonde locks, her slim curvy body with legs that go on for miles and breasts that make my mouth water. She's become my weakness and I have no idea how to make amends for my past sin…

It's been weeks since Reece left me without a backwards glance, and I'm an idiot because I'm finding it difficult to move on and forget him. It doesn't help that my best friend, Thalia, is engaged to his best friend, Phoenix. But tonight I intend to change all that and maybe do a little flirting with another guy and see where it leads…and who knows, it might even make the pain in my ass realize what he's missing…

Excerpt

"We're going to treat you right, but Callie – look at me."

I turn my head to look directly into Reece's eyes, which is easier said than done when he's standing to the side of me in jeans, looking heavily aroused, having removed his shirt and shoes.

"I need you to say it out loud so we both hear you. Are you sure you're okay being with us both?" He gently massages one of my nipples as Donovan reaches out doing the same to my other one, but my eyes stay focused on Reece.

He's asked me this three times already. "As I told you before, I'm sure. I've never been with two guys, but I read and it always sounds hot, so yeah, I want to know what it feels like having two cocks inside me at the same time."

"*Fuck*. I'm going to be coming in my jeans if you keep talking like that." Donovan groans as he unzips his jeans and shoves them down his legs. His swollen dick jerks now that it's free and points toward me.

These two delicious guys have me naked, sprawled out on my bed in my hotel, wet and aching, wishing they'd touch me between my legs as well as my breasts.

Hearing rustling, I turn my head to watch Reece. His back ripples as he leans over and slides his jeans from his legs. When he stands up, I gulp; he's huge! He's thick, long, and fucking pierced.

"You're pierced – that's hot."

He snickers and looks at Donovan. "Told you the chicks love it pierced."

"No fuckin' way is anyone coming near my dick with a needle."

I swivel my head back to Donovan and grin. He's covering his cock with his hands as though he expects someone to run at him and pierce him. My laughter soon turns to a groan as he starts to rub his hand up and down his length.

My eyes widen, but I'm unable to look away. Who knew it could be so damn hot to watch a guy touch himself.

"You like to watch?" He asks.

My gaze meets his lust filled eyes, but I can't keep it on his face as my gaze slips back to his hands and what they're doing. I feel the bed dip, which does distract me, more so, when I see Reece crawling on the bed between my thighs.

"I believe you said you want my mouth on you while Donovan sucks these gorgeous nipples." Reece rests his elbows on either side of me as he takes my generous breasts into his hands before leaning in and licking around each one of my nipples in turn.

My fingers slide over his smooth head, before I caress his face as I hold him to me. His cock is cradled against my pussy and with the pleasure he's creating with his hands, I can't stop arching against him.

"Mmm." He feels so good, and I can feel his cock pulsing against me with the wet tip. He's leaking with arousal, which is so hot, and has my pussy throbbing even more. I wiggle further into his embrace and wrap my legs around his hips.

"Oh, no," he groans breathing heavily. "I'm going down while Donovan moves in to play with these babies."

He kisses each of my nipples before leaving a trail of wet kisses down my stomach to my naked pussy. My legs fall from around him as I feel him spread me open.

"You're fucking gorgeous," he groans, and then leans in and kisses me at the apex of my thighs.

I nearly bolt from the bed, but Donovan's beside me, kneeling, holding me down, and looking ready to devour me.

He takes my face into his hands and seals our lips together. As he deepens the kiss between us, he reaches out with his hand and pinches one of my nipples. I pant in pleasure.

Between Reece kissing, licking and fucking me with his mouth and fingers, and having Donovan's hand on my nipple, his mouth locked on mine, I'm about to combust.

"So fucking tasty." Reece sucks my clit into his

mouth. "I can't get enough of you, baby." He feathers kisses along my groin and on top of my pussy before moving back to my core.

Needing to touch something, I reach out between Donovan's legs and make contact with his balls. He breaks from our kiss and cusses a blue streak while trying to catch his breath.

I squeeze lightly before stroking up to the tip of his cock, and rubbing his leaking essence around the mushroom head I feel a shudder of pleasure run through him. He's pulsing with want in my hand.

Lexi Buchanan can be found on the Web, Facebook, Goodreads, Amazon, Twitter and Google+

Soul-Mates Forever (Forever #3) by Vicki Green

Available on all major online retail retailers.

All Books in the series can be read as stand alones.

My Savior Forever (Forever #1) and Together Forever (Forever #2).

'Love …captures us in a moment and changes us forever'

When love isn't enough to break through the walls that were built so long ago, how is true happiness ever found? Paxton Davenport built these walls when every guy she met only wanted her gorgeous body. Her modeling career really takes off after returning to L.A. from her best friend's wedding. But her thoughts continually plague her of the hot rocker, Tucker Williams, who pursued her both times she visited her friend. Her rich parents have never provided the attention or love she needed growing up. She is considered your typical 21 year old rich bitch, snooty to most but deep inside she is the most loving and caring person you could ever know.

Tucker, or Tuck as everyone knows him, grew up in a house where a normal day was seeing his parents drugged out, no food to be found and finding solace in his guitar. His mom ending up in prison and his dad dying from an overdose leads him to falling in with the wrong crowd. With the help of friends, at the age of 22, he finds himself as a tattoo artist by day, the leader of a Rock band (Razers Edge) by night. He falls head over heels for Paxton one night when the band is playing at Barton's bar but she won't give him the time of day.

Will Tuck ever get through Paxton's walls or annoy the hell out of her trying?

Due to strong language and sexual content, this book is not intended for readers under the age of 18.

Social Media for Vicki Green Author

Website: http://www.vickigreenauthor.com/

Facebook page: https://www.facebook.com/VickiGreenAuthor

Twitter: @rileyks3

Goodreads Author: https://www.goodreads.com/author/show/7112966.Vicki_Green

Author page on Amazon: http://www.amazon.com/Vicki-Green/e/B00F2ZA9L8

MISSY JOHNSON

www.ingramcontent.com/pod-product-compliance
Lightning Source LLC
Chambersburg PA
CBHW032207190626
46810CB00019B/2157